*For Llewellyn
and Connie*

Acknowledgements

Background information for this story was gleaned from both primary and secondary sources found, among other places, at the American Antiquarian Society, the Massachusetts Historical Society, Harvard University, the Archives of the Commonwealth of Massachusetts, the New England Historic Genealogical Society, and the Hardwick and Brookfield Historical Societies. Of the many articles and books consulted, one of the most unusual was *Baroness von Riedesel and the American Revolution, Journal and Correspondence of a Tour of Duty 1776-1783* (Cary Memorial Library, Lexington, Massachusetts). The Journal provides a woman's eye-witness account of the retreat of Burgoyne's army after its defeat at Saratoga, written by the wife of General Friedrich Baron von Riedesel, Commander of a contingent of German mercenaries under General Burgoyne.

Many individuals have helped with the research for this book. One of the most important is Leon Thrasher of the Hardwick Historical Society, who introduced me to Bathsheba Ruggles Spooner in connection with my study of another Ruggles woman, Dr Mercy (Ruggles) Bisbee Jackson (1802-1877), Bathsheba's first cousin once removed. Since then, Leon has given frequent and generous help with archival material, and has put me in touch with others who have given invaluable assistance.

One such person, Robert Wilder of Brookfield, who has done extensive research on Joshua Spooner's house and barn, provided details about the Spooner property, as well as the topography of Brookfield in the late 18th century. He also furnished an account of his re-enactment of the trip made on foot by Buchanan, Brooks, and Ross from Brookfield to Worcester the night of the murder, using the route they would most likely have taken.

One morning in June, 1993, Edgar A. Whitcomb II, a local historian in West Boylston, helped me up a ladder to the dark attic of the town's Historical Museum, which had been an inn in 1778. There, with the aid of flood lamps, I had the privilege of studying haunting sketches scratched long ago onto the wooden walls. One of these curious works is a crude depiction of hangings that include details known to be associated with the executions for the Spooner murder. In November, 2002, Ed showed these images to my artist daughter, Constance Jennings Lane, who photographed them for the cover of this book. The title is Connie's copy of Bathsheba's signature as it appears on her letter to the Revolutionary Council, dated June 16, 1778 (Archives of the Commonwealth of Massachusetts).

Mrs Albert Anderson of Sandwich graciously gave me a tour through the historic home which she and her husband had restored. At the time of this story, it was the Newcomb Tavern, owned by Bathsheba's mother, where Bathsheba lived until she was eight years old.

I owe a great deal to Barbara Trippel Simmons, Sidney E. Berger, and Thomas Knowles, Curators of Manuscripts at the American Antiquarian Society in Worcester, who, over the course of several years, made available the Society's archives concerning many aspects of the Spooner murder case, and answered many questions.

Edward W. Hanson, Associate Editor of the Massachusetts Historical Society, sent me a photocopy of Robert Treat Paine's "The Minutes of Trial and Law Cases," which includes his account of the Spooner murder trial, for which he was the prosecuting lawyer in his capacity as Attorney General of the fledgling State of Massachusetts Bay. The other account on which I relied was a compilation of notes written by the Honorable Jedadiah Foster (see *American Criminal Trials* by Peleg W. Chandler, Boston, Charles C. Little and James Brown, 1844).

Reference Librarians at the Massachusetts Archives on Columbia Point, Boston, helped me locate records relative to the trial and execution of Bathsheba and the soldiers.

Beverly H. Osborne, Librarian at the Worcester Historical Museum, provided information about the Green Estate, home of Bathsheba's sister Mary after she married John Green. Ms Osborne also tracked down what was happening in the Worcester County Sheriff's office during the period between March and July, 1778.

Jacqueline C. Tidman, Local History Librarian at the Westborough Public Library furnished archival material concerning the Reverend Ebenezer Parker, whose execution sermon (Parker Family Papers, 1707-1810, #1932, American Antiquarian Society) was full of fire and brimstone, directed mainly at Bathsheba.

Mariam Touba, Newspaper Librarian at the New York Historical Society, searched for reports of the Spooner murder in 1778 New York newspapers, and found none, thus supporting the notion, frequently voiced over more than two centuries, that Bathsheba's father, Brigadier General Timothy Ruggles, then in New York, knew nothing about his daughter's involvement in the murder until much later.

J. B. Cahill, Manuscript Archivist at the Public Archives in Nova Scotia, provided information about the Brigadier and his sons after they moved to Nova Scotia.

Mirium Robles at the Registry of the Probate Court in Worcester and Vincent McCaughey, Attorney, supplied copies of documents relative to the administration of Joshua Spooner's estate.

Mr R. A. Lovell, author of *Sandwich, a Cape Cod Town* (1989), shared the results of his considerable research on the Brigadier and his family, as well as Joshua Spooner's genealogy, which he had carefully worked out.

Nina Groves of Milton, Massachusetts, an authority on Governor Thomas Hutchinson, took me and my husband on a walking tour of the land that once constituted the Governor's country estate in Milton.

Dr Mary Ellen Avery, Thomas Morgan Rotch Professor of Pediatrics at the Harvard Medical School, gave advice concerning childhood illnesses which would surely have been fatal in the eighteenth century, thereby helping me give a credible account of Baby John's death.

During the course of my research, I met Deborah Navas who later published an article and a book about the Spooner case. For years, we have shared information.

Friends in a writers' workshop in Duxbury, Massachusetts taught me valuable lessons about writing fiction. I especially owe a debt of gratitude to Priscilla Weld and Robert Hale.

By far the most important contributor to this work is my daughter, Constance Jennings Lane, whose inestimable contribution is mentioned in my Author's Note. Without her help, this book would never have been written. And it would not have been published without the constant support and encouragement of my husband, Addison Llewellyn Jennings, who also undertook the tedious task of copy editing the text..

Thanks to all of you.

Author's Note

In the spring of 1778, seven people were arrested for the brutal murder of Joshua Spooner. Four were brought to trial, and on Thursday, July 2, 1778, three soldiers and Joshua's pregnant wife, Bathsheba Ruggles Spooner, were hanged in Worcester, Massachusetts.

Sometime in the late 1980s, my daughter, Constance Jennings Lane, and I ran across tales about the crime and began serious research concerning it. Archives in various Massachusetts libraries yielded the salient facts surrounding the murder, information about Joshua and his family, and even more about the Ruggles family. Bathsheba's father, Timothy Ruggles, was a prominent, wealthy Tory involved in pre-Revolutionary Massachusetts politics; her mother, descended from Mayflower Pilgrims John Howland and Elizabeth Tilly, was the daughter of Judge Melatiah Bourne (1674-1742), probably the wealthiest man in Sandwich in his day. Because Bathsheba was a Tory whose trial was set in a highly charged Whig environment, we became convinced that political considerations played a role in her conviction. We therefore took a careful look at Massachusetts history and politics during the period from 1765 (The Stamp Act) until 1778.

Archives, however, revealed little about Bathsheba, the woman, her character, or motives for the crime, except for legendary conjecture, much of which reflected anti-Tory sentiments. She left no diary, no letters. We have only scraps of her alleged remarks, gleaned from contemporary newspaper reports and from *The Dying Declaration* of the three soldiers who were ultimately executed with her. Letters written by the Reverend Thaddeus Maccarty, Bathsheba's spiritual advisor, as well as his execution sermon, provided a few other valuable clues, and, with these threads of evidence, Connie and I began the long process of creating Bathsheba and exploring possible motives strong enough to bring her together with five men, all focused on getting rid of Joshua Spooner.

Eventually, Connie dropped out of the project for lack of time as she pursued a career in art while raising three daughters with her husband. I, therefore, am responsible for what is written here, although much of it incorporates her contributions, both her ideas and occasionally even her wording.

I have tried to be true to recorded facts about the case and have included historical information important to the understanding of the story. All the characters except Rebecca and Mrs Harding actually existed, but they are endowed with imagined characteristics, except for those people about whom much could be found—for example, Bathsheba's father, Brigadier General Timothy Ruggles, and Robert Treat Paine. Although the love story between Nathan Danforth (Jonathan Danforth in real life) and Bathsheba is fictional, it certainly could have happened; he did in fact marry one of her cousins in 1780, after the death of his first wife Susanna.

In short, the book is an attempt, through fiction, to make sense of a puzzling crime that for centuries has captured the imagination of people in central Massachusetts.

BATHSHUA

Prologue

July 2, 1778
Worcester, Massachusetts

An impatient crowd, five thousand strong, clogged the dusty, hot, fly-ridden streets. Some families from distant towns had spent the night in open fields beneath a threatening sky. Others had risked fleas in local homes, sharing beds with youngsters whose parents had been quick to see a chance to turn a profit. Those few with a pocket full of money had lodged somewhat more comfortably at Brown's or Walker's Tavern, where they bought drinks for regulars in exchange for sensational reports about the crime.

On a hillock near the outskirts of the town, four farmers, proud of their commission from the sheriff, were raising the scaffold. Vendors were setting up their stalls along the road—"Hard cider, tuppence a large mug!" "Gingerbread!" "Rum, here, beer, near-beer!" The shouts of urchins, scattered among the crowd, added to the din, "A Mournful Poem. Only a shilling for a Mournful Poem, direct from Isaiah Thomas' press!"

Its final quatrain summed up twenty-two stern verses:

And let this Warning Loud and Shrill
Be heard by Everyone,
O do no more such Wickedness
As has of late been Done

At half past two, a dirge began to toll from the steeple of the Old South Church. A pale woman sat beside the Reverend Maccarty as his chaise jolted slowly over ruts in the open field. Behind them three

1

male prisoners followed a horse drawn cart burdened with four pine coffins.

The heavens darkened as the procession, under the guard of a hundred militiamen, neared the place of execution. Horses neighed, and officers hallooed. "MAKE WAY! MAKE WAY!"

The woman appeared calm and unafraid, although occasionally she flinched, as if suffering from a deep internal stab. When the gallows came in view, the Reverend asked if the sight did not appall her. She answered, no.

Dry lightning flashed across the sky as Sheriff Greenleaf stepped up to the Reverend's chaise. Whispers flew through the crowd that perhaps at the last minute Mrs Spooner was going to be let off. But the sheriff was merely exempting her from the regulation that required a criminal to stand during the reading of the death warrant.

Greenleaf motioned the men to ascend the stage, then followed them. His voice, as he delivered the words that authorized the taking of four lives, was scarcely audible beneath the sterile thunder.

When he finished, he gave a nod to Mrs Spooner. With the Reverend's help, she descended from the chaise, and, after bidding him goodbye, crept up the thirteen steps. When she reached the top, she managed to stand tall and face the sheriff, and before he pinioned her, she took his hand. "Sir, I am ready." The tremor in her voice reflected her physical distress. "In a little time I expect to be in bliss, although a few years might elapse before I see you and my other friends again." He hooded her. She spoke again. "This is the happiest day I ever saw. I have no doubt it will be well with me."

The sheriff unfolded a large, black handkerchief, raised it, then let it fall. Within seconds, the stage was dropped, and the prisoners were swinging from their broken necks, twisting silhouettes against a sky lit white by lightening.

Chapter 1

Middle Massachusetts
1765

Bathsheba knelt beside the stream that marked the southern boundary of her father's large estate. Flushed from the heavy August heat, she cupped her hands, filled them with the cool, clear water, and lowered her face. Bridie drank noisily nearby. Bathsheba waited for her mare to finish, then rose and stroked the animal's neck. "Beauty," she said. "Good horse." Bridie answered with a nod and whiney.

That morning, Bathsheba had risen early, relieved to escape her unsettling dreams; nonetheless, disturbing images still swarmed in her head. As was her wont when she needed consolation, she went to Bridie. Cantering through the countryside always helped, but today the oppressive heat soon forced her to turn back and seek the quiet shade beside the stream, her special private place where she often came to read or muse.

Her father, returned from Boston the evening before, had provided much to think about. He had been weary from his journey of fifty miles or so, but not too tired to unload the latest news. His family, like everyone in Massachusetts, had been hearing rumors for days, and they gathered around him, eager for his first hand account.

He didn't mince his words. The Stamp Act, he fumed, was causing men to lose their heads, and Boston was fast becoming an unsafe town. Dependent for law and order on just the sheriff and the few doddering old men on the night watch, it was falling into a state of anarchy.

Less than two weeks ago, Andrew Oliver, appointed by the Crown as a stamp distributor, had suffered personal abuse and senseless, serious loss of property. The mob—Sam Adams must have been behind it—had hanged him in effigy on a giant elm at the corner of Newbury and Essex Streets, the so-called Liberty Tree, a rallying place for the so-called Patriots. Attached to the dummy were both an insulting inscription and a couplet, easy to remember; here it is: "What greater Joy did ever New England see/ Than a Stampman hanging from a Tree." Not only that; beside him was a large boot with the Devil crawling out: Lord Bute, of course, the poor devil whom the ill-informed rabble believed to be the author of the Stamp Act. Mistaken fools!

Governor Bernard demanded that the sheriff cut down the offensive images, but of course nothing came of that. So Bernard called a meeting of his Council. Back and forth, this or that, what to do? The debate went on till nightfall. Meanwhile the mob of its own accord yanked down the effigies and started marching them around the Town House, then through the building, right past the Council Chambers, defiant. From there, they swept down King Street to Oliver's Dock and hacked down a brand new building, which, they assumed, Andrew Oliver had built to house the stamps. Wrong again; hoodlums never bother about facts.

They loaded the wreckage onto carts and headed for Fort Hill, stopping on the way at Oliver's house long enough to chop off the head of his effigy and hurl stones through his windows. When they tired of that, they charged up the hill to start a bonfire with the wood from his demolished shop. Yelling like maniacs, they tossed the headless dummy on the flames and, drinking toasts to Oliver's demise, they watched it writhe and shrivel. Then back to his place to wreak more havoc there. They smashed his fence and outhouses, trashed his garden, broke into his house and destroyed his furniture, shouting all the while that they were out to kill him.

"Which they most certainly would have done if he had not already fled." The Brigadier gave his ivory headed cane a sharp rap on the floor.

The following day, under further threats that terrified his wife and children, Oliver gave in to the tipsy horde and promised to resign as stamp distributor. What else could he do?

The Brigadier brought his fist down on the table. "That's what these self-styled Patriots, backed by Adams, that's what they did to a

4

man who has been one of the best public servants Massachusetts has ever had, never a friend of the Stamp Act, accusations to the contrary, no more than I. They're beginning to call themselves 'Sons of Liberty.' 'Sons of Violence' would be more fitting." Then, under his breath, "Sons of bitches!"

All this was bad enough, but it was her father's description of the most recent night of terror that most disturbed Bathsheba. He had been caught on the fringes yesterday, Monday evening, when the rioters started up again, making their first stop at the rented quarters of the Commissioner of Customs. The landlord told them that Charles Paxton wasn't home, and—a cagey man, that one—he invited the entire mob to be his guests at the nearby tavern. A glass or two of sillibub all round blurred their focus, and, forgetting about Paxton, they surged down the street to ax the doors of William Story, smash his windows, enter and burn all the official records he'd amassed as Deputy Registrar of the Admiralty Court.

Then on to Benjamin Hallowell's place to reduce to ashes his accounts as Comptroller of the Customs, not to mention gutting his well stocked cellar.

Once all these lesser appointees of the Crown had been taken care of, Ebenezer Mackintosh—Sam Adams' man, you can bet—gave the signal to swing on to Garden Court Street and the biggest prize of all, the Lieutenant Governor's beautiful ancestral home. "It distresses me to speak of it," the Brigadier said.

Bells rang, horns blatted, men shouted like demented savages. Hutchinson, at supper with his children, ordered them to flee, but his daughter Sally would not budge without him. They both finally ducked through the back garden, and, by God, not a moment too soon.

"The hellish crew fell on his house with the rage of devils." The Brigadier wavered between fury and sadness. "They axed down the door. Some scrambled to the roof and began beating down the cupola and stripping slate. Others filled the rooms below or stayed outside to plunder in the gardens."

Not content with tearing off the wainscot and the hangings, they rampaged throughout the night, splitting doors, smashing furniture and pictures, slashing mattresses and curtains, leaving rubble two feet deep, feathers, shards of china, shredded rugs, and fallen plaster. Only the approaching dawn and heavy rain prevented total demolition of the building.

The garden fence lay flat; the trees, a century's growth, now mangled branches strewn across the lawn. "Such ruins were never before seen in America," the Brigadier said. "That's what my friend Hutchinson said to me this morning as we stood gazing at the wreckage. Emboldened by the wine they'd hauled up from his cellar, the marauders stole his plate, defaced his family portraits, took all the clothes from every closet, the servants' not excepted, and, to boot, they pocketed £900 sterling.

"They left not a single book. They scattered or destroyed all the manuscripts and papers Hutchinson had been collecting for over 30 years, including the public records in his custody. As I stood with him this morning, appalled, stunned, without words, his neighbor, the Reverend Eliot, approached and handed him the sodden manuscript of his *History of Massachusetts*. 'I found it in the gutter,' Eliot said."

Bathsheba had never seen her father so upset, so saddened. He usually reacted to injustice with righteous anger and some plan, some countermeasure, but now, when he finished telling, he simply shook his head and walked away. She understood. The Brigadier, a man of action, had been helpless to protect his friends, and he would be helpless to protect his family, should it come to that. Bathsheba had been weaned on politics, her parents talked it all the time, and she was an eager listener. She had reason to believe her father when he said that, although there was as yet no violence in the countryside, the forces of revolt might soon reach from Boston inland. If that happened, he surely would be targeted, his estate, his person, his family. Should Adams' followers infiltrate from Boston, no confidant of the Lieutenant Governor, no man who supported the interests of the Crown, would escape.

But Bathsheba knew that no matter what might happen, her father would never hide his Loyalist leanings. As Hardwick's representative to the General Court, he would stand up for his beliefs. He flew a

British flag from a pole in the field where once a year he entertained his neighbors with a New England bull fight, followed by games and a sumptuous barbecue. Brigadier General Timothy Ruggles would refuse to be intimidated, even on pain of death, and fortunately, for now at least, Hardwick was not like Boston, and the Brigadier's constituents were as loyal to him as he was to their King. They knew he was as staunch an American as ever lived, a man who believed that the well-being of the colonies required protection by the mother country. He understood the intrigues going on in Europe, France and Spain eyeing the rich lands across the sea, ready to pounce at any sign of British weakness. Hardwick voters liked the way he handled things, which was why they had been sending him for years to represent them in the General Court. Moreover, although he was a graduate of Harvard College, a lawyer and a judge and the wealthiest man in Worcester County, he dealt with all men as his equal.

Bathsheba was proud to be his daughter.

She was about to mount her mare when she became aware of someone approaching from the open field behind her. She turned, and her smile accentuated the sharp angles of her face, which, combined with her dusky skin, dark eyes, and jet-black hair, prompted people to remark in whispers that somewhere, a few generations past, there must have been an Indian. But of course that couldn't be. Her pedigree was flawless, going back on her mother's side to the first arrivals on the Mayflower, and almost as far back on her father's. Still, she unquestionably had about her a native look—stunning, really.

She dropped Bridie's reins and hurried to meet Nathan. How handsome he is! His rugged features, his blousy shirt, full sleeves, open at the neck, reminded her a little of her father. He hadn't had the opportunity to go to college, and he had no flare for politics, but he was salt of the earth, as brother Richard put it. She admired his independent, quick intelligence, his skill at farming, and his shrewd management of Hardwick's General Store. Just being near him made her happy. "How did you know I was here?"

7

"Just a guess. You often come here when you are upset." He opened his arms to receive her. "Richard told me the news your father brought."

It was so like Nathan to seek her out. They had known each other since she was eight, when her family arrived in Hardwick from Sandwich on Cape Cod. He had soon become her brother Richard's closest friend, and hers as well. Of late, however, their affection for each other had crossed the bounds of friendship.

"Papa tells things vividly," she said. Despite the heat, she gave a little shiver. "Oh, I'm not afraid. Don't think that." She was silent for a moment, then, "Sally saved her father's life." Sally Hutchinson was not much older than Bathsheba and already mistress in her father's house, taking her mother's place since her illness and untimely death. Sally moved in exciting, sophisticated circles. "Sally acts as hostess when her father entertains."

Nathan nodded. "Aye, but it's safer here."

Bathsheba shrugged. "The rioting, where will it end?" She expected Nathan to have an answer, and she knew he wouldn't put her down, he wouldn't tell her she was just a girl who shouldn't bother her head about such matters.

"Your father might soon be in trouble."

She considered for a moment, then, "Yes. Perhaps he already is."

The Brigadier had been chosen by the General Court to go, come October, to New York as one of Massachusetts' representatives at the Stamp Act Congress to discuss the crisis.

Risky business for a Loyalist in 1765.

Chapter 2

After a month of vacillations and negotiations, the Brigadier, urged on—ordered, really—by Royal Governor Bernard, departed for New York despite his better judgment. The weather, which had been foul for days, matched his mood. "No good will come of this," he growled. The Congress was James Otis's idea, and he would be there, which was why Governor Bernard insisted that the Brigadier should be there too. "Someone has to argue on our side," Bernard had said at their last interview. "You're the only one who can keep those firebrands at bay." So the Brigadier agreed to go; it was his duty.

Bathsheba rode a few miles with her father, then said goodbye, good luck. Back at the house, she stopped by his study, gathered up the untidy pile of newspapers and curled up in his chair. But the light was dim and she soon wearied of reading the harangue in the *Gazette* against the Stamp Act. Lulled by the lazy fire, she drew a shawl around her shoulders and watched the branches of the great oak bend and quiver in the wind. A bird escaped from the tree and disappeared into the distance, blurred by rivulets of water streaming down the pane. Bathsheba drifted into a dream—her father making some important speech, her mother resolute and critical behind him. He faltered, and she herself took a stand beside him and faced a cursing crowd. She was about to speak when the sharp crack of a breaking branch startled her awake.

By the middle of October, Indian summer had set in. Nathan came early on the morning of the Hardwick Fair, and Bathsheba watched as he helped scrub a pair of Richard's piglets for the competition. Afterwards they chose samples of her father's fruit, which she arranged in wicker baskets for display at the horticultural booth. As

Nathan handed her a rose-flecked pear, their fingers touched, and she bent closer for a kiss.

He reminded her about the party. "Tonight. A house warming, sort of. I think you'll like the place. At least it's mine, all clear, no mortgage. Nothing formal, but there'll be dancing and good food and drink. My sister Liz is helping."

Bathsheba had not forgotten.

They walked hand in hand down the path leading through the meadow to the Common. Halfway, Nathan stopped beneath a vivid maple tree, and put down the picnic hamper. The message in his eyes was clear, but just as she was moving closer, a neighbor came in view, riding towards them at a clip and shattering the moment. "Hello, hello. A glorious day. I'll see you there."

The Common was festooned with British flags. Girls in large bonnets bedecked with pastel ribbons, were flirting with each other's beaus, and small boys were chasing little girls as they waited for the Punch and Judy show to start. Their mothers, cradling babies in their arms, were gossiping nearby, with one eye on their toddlers. A few young men were idling near the roped-off space where wrestlers were preparing for their matches, while others, standing by their animals, were sizing up their competition. Someone was organizing a game of quoits.

Nathan and Bathsheba stopped at a refreshment booth. "How about some ale?" he asked.

She smiled, teasing. "Papa says that alcohol can make a fool of you."

"Aye. Look at that one over there." He pointed to a beggar, singing off-key unsteadily, a flask in one hand, a dirty kerchief in the other. After each swig, he shouted "God save the King!" and bent over in a wobbly bow.

They paid a penny to play a game of darts, and Nathan signed up for a one-legged race. He won, and Bathsheba crowned him with his prize, a Nipmuck Indian headband from which two eagle feathers dangled.

They found a shady spot near the podium and, while they picnicked on their chicken, bread and cider, they listened to endless speeches by Select Men. Judging by the speakers' praise of English customs, one would never guess that Bostonians, no more than fifty miles away, were busy denouncing everything the British did.

Now some magistrate was making reference to her father, and her attention sharpened. "Let us not forget Tim Ruggles, our friend and neighbor who can't be with us on this festive day. Let us not forget that it was he who started, by a Resolution in the House three years ago, this wonderful tradition, the Hardwick Fair, patterned, Ladies and Gentlemen, on the country fairs in England." Bathsheba squeezed Nathan's hand and joined the chorus of "Hear! Hear!"

The judges started to give out the prizes, and Richard's piglets squealed and wiggled when held high for everyone to see as he accepted their blue ribbons. Nathan nudged Bathsheba and pointed to an enclosure where Parson Maxwell's goat, that hadn't won a thing, was munching on a judge's hat, left hanging on a post. Friends stopped to talk. "Don't seem quite the same without your father running things." "Too bad he couldn't be here." "But maybe he can set things straight down in New York."

Bathsheba nodded. "Maybe."

That evening, Nathan's sister Liz had everything in readiness. The chairs in the parlor were lined up along the wall to make room for dancing, and food was laid out in the sitting room. "You look lovely, dear," Liz said.

Nathan took Bathsheba by the hand and escorted her around his house. "Like it?" he asked.

"Oh, yes. Yes, Nathan." Yet she could not help noticing the differences between her father's house and this place where she might someday live. Here the rooms were plain, no French wallpaper depicting some ancient allegory, no japanned highboy, no gold-framed mirror above the fireplace. And Nathan's Windsor chairs had not come from Newport. But such things don't matter.

He guided her outside. "I'll wager we won't have another night like this before the cold sets in," he said. The moon was rising, and he drew her close. But before he could improve on his advantage, a gig drew up, the first guests called out their greetings, and his duties as a host began.

While Liz bustled, making certain everything was right, Bathsheba stood with Nathan near the door, her imagination soaring. This is how it's going to be someday, she thought, she and Nathan welcoming their guests, their house overflowing with their friends. The thought excited her, but still, she wondered, just a little. She shared her father's expensive tastes. She was proud that the grounds of his estate were equal to those of any lord in England, with a 20 acre deer park and extensive orchards of exotic hybrid fruits. His pack of hunting hounds and stable of thirty thoroughbred horses were a delight to friends who sometimes visited for weeks. She glanced at Nathan, handsome and reliable, and wished for a moment, just a moment, that he was also rich and dazzlingly exciting.

Chapter 3

In the shadows at the back of the house, a young man was removing small chests of tea from his saddlebags and stacking them beneath the lantern in the lean-to. When he finished, he stood back and withdrew a pipe from the pocket of his vest. He had no means to light it, but it brought him pleasure anyway as his thumb stroked the full breasts of the mermaid carved around the bowl. The curves and textures of the polished meerschaum aroused him.

Attracted by the gaiety drifting from open windows, the tradesman approached the house. The gig was ending with applause all round and calls for a contredanse. He stopped near the barberry bush on the south side of the house, where he could watch the party without being seen. Of course, instead of lurking there, he could knock, announce that he'd delivered the order, and wait to be invited in. Nathan Danforth would give him a warm welcome, he was sure—a genial fellow, Danforth, rather handsome in his rustic way. But he wasn't in the mood for Danforth and his crowd. Not tonight. Instead, he'd watch the dancing for a minute and then move on to something sportier.

He exchanged his pipe for his pocket-flask and was raising it when he paused midway, taken by a most agreeable surprise. There, directly in his line of vision, at the center of a semicircle of regrouping guests, was—well, how should one put it? She's a beauty, nothing short of a perfect jewel. See how she touches Danforth's sleeve, looking as if she has a purpose. What a tantalizing blend of innocence and daring! There is something maverick about her, a cross between a tomboy and a princess, unquestionably a challenge.

He took a swig of rum and stepped a little closer, being careful to keep out of sight.

What the fiddler lacked in expertise he made up in energy, and the pace was fast. She dances superbly, the observer thought as he fondled his mermaid. And one can't deny that Danforth is her match—a disconcerting observation. She was clearly fashioned by the gods for a much finer lover.

The music stopped, and the fiddler indicated he was going to take a break. She was moving close to Nathan, whispering something in his ear. A secret, perhaps? She slipped her arm through his and let him lead her, laughing, through the front hall, past the open door. Now Liz, the spinster sister—the observer knew her slightly: an unattractive wench—approached her brother, spoke to him briefly, and he went off, no doubt to the kitchen on some errand.

Liz turned to welcome someone who had just arrived, a handsome woman, fashionably dressed in Boston style. They conversed and Liz nodded, pointing after Danforth. The Bostonian smiled her thanks and hurried off.

Nathan's gem of a partner, stranded, was showing obvious displeasure, scowling, her eyes burning with annoyance. The observer grinned, and nodded to himself. He stepped back into the shadows, and, feeling that fortune was about to smile on him, he decided he should tarry here a little longer.

Liz took her place beside the flip bowl, ladled a little of the fiery drink into a lady's flip glass, and passed it to Bathsheba. "Are they really true, the reports about the rioting in Boston?" she asked. "What does your father say?" Liz, like most Hardwick people, valued the Brigadier's opinion. And his daughter was sure to know the ins and outs of what was going on in Boston. Most unusual for a girl, people said, rather like her mother.

"Papa says he's never seen the town as tense as it has been these past few months." It took some effort to be gracious, she was so riled with Nathan, and when Liz asked about the Stamp Act Congress in New York, Bathsheba said she had nothing to report about her father's business there. "He never writes. Besides, I'm sure you've heard that everything is secret." For a moment she was tempted to mention how worried he had been before he left, how he'd told her he expected trouble. But he would not approve of her going on like that, and, anyway, she really didn't want to talk about the Stamp Act, or the Congress, or Sam Adams, or James Otis, or the troubles of the Lieutenant Governor, or anything related to the riots – not now. "Do you know when Nathan will be finished with whatever he is doing?" she asked. But Liz was turning to another guest.

Never mind, being unattended was not without advantages. Young men, most of whom Bathsheba had known since they were little boys, gathered around her, murmuring compliments: she looked ravishing; would she be a partner for the next dance? her gown was perfect. It was indeed, and she had chosen it especially for Nathan.

She put down her glass, excused herself, and headed toward the kitchen. She opened the door a crack, enough to see Nathan sitting at the table opposite the Boston woman. She must be twice my age, Bathsheba thought. They were holding hands and talking earnestly, and she was thanking him for seeing her alone. She needed his advice about some thing or other. She glanced up, saw Bathsheba, and looked right through her.

I've seen that look before, Bathsheba thought. She remembered now. She had met Widow Mary Jackson a year or so ago, when they ran into each other quite by chance at Nathan's store. And she looked right through me then with her confident, superior glance that made me feel that I could never know or understand the fast, complicated world in which she lives. Nathan had explained that Mary had come from Boston to visit Liz. They had been close friends in the days before Mary took a husband and left Hardwick.

Perhaps!

The fiddler was starting up again. Bathsheba closed the kitchen door, slipped to the side entrance, and went outside. She sat down on the bench beneath the arbor to sort out all she knew about this Widow Jackson. Not that it made any difference, really. It was just that she would like to see the picture as a whole, know where she stood. She recalled that brother Richard, who sometimes went to Boston with Nathan to help lay in stocks for the general store, had met Mary more than once. "She runs the *Brazen Head* in Cornhill," he had reported.

"She trades in everything from powder and gun shot to pork. She's a tinker, too. Makes pots and pans or anything a client wants. A bouncy lass, with a head for figures and a heart for fun."

An independent woman—the kind Nathan likes. One of his most endearing traits had always been his open admiration of her own independent spirit. Not every man counted such an attitude a virtue in a woman, and she usually tried to tone it down. But with Nathan she could feel free. However, in this matter of independence, she was no match for Mary Jackson. Not good. Of course, it didn't matter, not a whit, it was just that she couldn't tolerate the thought.

She was musing on ways she might confront this threat, when a soft "Hello" gave her a start. She turned to see a young man leaning against a tree near the corner of the house, and although she could barely see his face, she could make out that he was tall and slight. The bright moonlight played on the velvet of his vest as he approached her, slowly. Then, standing before her, legs astride, arms crossed, he looked her over as though he was appraising a fine animal.

All thoughts of Nathan and Mary Jackson skyrocketed away. Bathsheba caught her breath. The stranger's appearance was arresting. His long auburn hair was tied in a queue behind. His high cheekbones and strong chin alone were enough to make his face distinctive. But it was his eyes that captivated her, dark eyes that caressed her. His smile was odd, not quite a smile, mysterious.

"Do you have a license for your looks, miss?" His voice was silk. "Beauty like yours should be controlled."

Her instincts told her she should leave, and she stood up. "I don't remember that we've met," she said. "Do I know you?"

He came close enough for her to see his slender fingers fondling the mermaid on his pipe. She looked away.

"Such craving for detail," he said. "My name is Spooner, Joshua Spooner." He pocketed his pipe and carefully arranged his wrist lace. "I'm a trader among other things, recently removed from Boston to my new place in Brookfield. I came by just now with a delivery of Bohea, top grade from China, for Danforth's store. I hesitated to disturb him at his party, so I left the tea out in the lean-to. And you are?"

He raised his eyebrows as she introduced herself. "Is that right?" he said. "Brigadier Ruggles' daughter. You and your father are both legends around here, you know. I've heard say that you're as high-spirited as he is, and as smart."

She knew the pleasure she was taking in his flattery was inappropriate. She stepped a little closer.

"I'm amazed you're here alone," he said. "I would have thought you'd be surrounded by admirers." Then that mysterious smile again. "I should not have been surprised to find you out here in the moonlight holding hands with someone special. Stealing a kiss or two?"

Outrageous!

"Why don't you come out for a ride with me?"

She looked at him in disbelief.

"I have a splendid horse, just brought in from Rhode Island."

She couldn't take her eyes off him.

"It's a perfect night for a bit of an adventure, eh? I can see you are intrigued."

"Oh, no. I just came out to take the air." He grasped both her hands, and his eyes lingered over every detail of her features, stirring an intense response.

Bewitched.

"Nothing to fear. I'm just offering to escort you home." He paused. "I noticed Danforth's sister Liz is at the party. She knows me. Go tell her you aren't feeling well, you aren't accustomed to the flip, and it has made you dizzy and light-headed." He led her through the shadows toward his horse. "Tell her that you met me in the garden where you were resting for a moment, feeling a little ill and thinking you should leave, go home. Tell her that I'm going past your place and have offered you a lift. That way there'll be no fuss. She'll appreciate your thoughtfulness. Go on, go tell Liz."

What harm could come of that? How foolish to argue with Nathan's friend, clearly a distinguished gentleman. It was quite natural he should offer to accompany her home. And it was true that she felt dizzy and light-headed, although she knew that it was not the flip.

"Hurry," Joshua called softly as she headed toward the house.

The fields were still and white beneath the harvest moon. Joshua drank occasionally from his pocket flask, each time offering Bathsheba some. She made no effort to refuse. When they reached her father's deer park, he dismounted. "Let's walk awhile," he said. She hesitated, pushing back a wave of apprehension, but when he reached up, she let him take her from his horse. They proceeded slowly. Now and then a squirrel or rabbit scuttled across their path, or a startled doe crashed through the underbrush.

They lingered on the bridge where the stream was wide, and watched the quivering reflection of the moon. "Like moonlight on the Thames, would you say?" he asked.

"In London, you mean?"

"Of course. Have you never been to England?"

"I've only been as far as Boston, and that only once or twice." London!

"You need a little more adventure in your life." He took her hand and she let his fingers intertwine with hers. The lonely sounds of nocturnal insects and the intoxicating scent of some late-blooming plant intensified the aura that surrounded them. Although she had often flirted, and sometimes kissed, it had never been like this. She came close, she let go, she lost herself.

Then suddenly a diffuse but real sense of danger set off an alarm. She pulled back. "Thank you for bringing me this far," she said. "But I'd rather go the rest alone." When he started to object, she shook her head. "No, please. Please let me go."

"Tomorrow I'll pay a formal call," he called to her as he turned to walk back to his horse. Perfect, he told himself, swollen with anticipation. So marvelously untouched.

Chapter 4

At first, the morning seemed like any other hazy autumn morning. Through the open window came the faint, familiar sounds of cowbells and the gentle mooing from the herd in the back pasture. Although not yet quite awake, Bathsheba recognized her mother's voice, going over the work that needed to be done before the Brigadier got back, telling brother Timothy not to forget to mend the railing on the bridge across the stream.

Jolted to full consciousness by mention of the bridge, Bathsheba sat up and squinted through the sunlight slanting across the counterpane. Her throat was dry and a dull ache snaked around inside her head. She, who had never been uncertain about anything, was waking up to a barrage of doubts. Just where did last night's adventure leave her? Having encouraged Mr Spooner—yes, that was the word for it, encouraged him—was she now obliged by common decency to cast her lot with him? Did kissing the way they'd kissed demand commitment? And Nathan, what of him?

Mr Spooner, an experienced, worldly man, had lavished her with compliments and met her lips in a most disturbing way. He was irresistible, yet she knew nothing about him, really, except that he was obviously a gentleman. Her thoughts kept skidding. One moment she wished she'd never met him, the next, she was trembling at the thought of seeing him again.

She rose and gazed into her narrow looking glass. Her appearance was the same as on any other morning, but she felt different. She let her shift slip from her shoulders and stood naked, facing her image, seeing herself in a new way. She poured water from the porcelain pitcher into the flowered bowl and bathed. What was she to do? What stance ought she to take? Mr Spooner's parting words persisted. "I'll pay a formal call," he'd said. "Tomorrow." And now tomorrow was today, and he might be here within the hour. She must not meet him like a stammering schoolgirl not knowing her own mind.

"I will refuse to see him," she said out loud as she began to dress. But what if she could not refuse, what if she didn't have the will? A foolish thought! She had always had the will to do whatever she decided she would do. But now, just the idea of Mr Spooner knocking and entering and tempting her again threw her off balance. Maybe it would help to talk with someone.

Her thoughts turned to the person who had listened to her troubles since she was a child and who never failed to keep her secrets. She stopped in the kitchen for some strong black coffee, then went out to the stables. "I'm going to New Braintree," she told the stable boy as she saddled her mare. "What do *you* think, Bridie?" she murmured as she stroked the animal, her confidante since her sixteenth birthday, the best present Papa ever gave. "Bridie, what should I do?" she asked, as if addressing a close friend.

She found her Uncle John kneeling on a cushion in his garden, where an orange quilt of red and yellow leaves covered his perennial beds. "I'm planting tulip bulbs," he explained, his round face shining with the pleasure he was taking in her unexpected visit.

She bent down and kissed him. "Why so dressed up?"

He was wearing the cambric jacket she had embroidered with red roses for his thirty-third birthday. Her father's youngest sibling, John was nearer her age than his brother's, and he adored her.

"I dress properly," he said solemnly, "because I want the flowers to respect me."

"But why so deep? They won't be able to come up."

"You're wrong, Shua. They could force their way from China when the sun beats hot next spring. I plant them deep to keep them safe." The sunlight at his back made a halo of his curls. "Secure from squirrels and naughty field mice. But what brings you here? You haven't ridden all the way from Hardwick just to watch me garden."

She knelt to help him. "You know I always love to see you."

When the last bulb was in the ground, Uncle John fetched his ancient sprinkling can and watered, then suggested that they go inside. "I'll make some scones, my special blend, the kind you've always liked the best."

While he mixed the flour and sugar, she told him what had happened, more or less. "I've never met a man like Mr Spooner," she said. "I guess that you could say he swept me off my feet." Her uncle looked surprised. "But you mustn't think it was against my will," she added.

She paused, expectant. If he would say something, anything, it would make things easier. She tried another tack. "Mr Spooner questioned me about Lieutenant Governor Hutchinson. Everybody in the world seems to be aware that he is Papa's friend. Mr Spooner said that Mr Hutchinson's a relative of his, going way back, he said. That would interest Papa, don't you think?"

Uncle John looked doubtful.

"For months I've been falling in love with Nathan, and he with me. Now this. Please say something. Help me."

Uncle John placed the dough in his brick oven, then led her to his secret chamber, the room she always begged to see when she was little, the room where mystery and knowledge met. She loved the brilliant jungle scenes he had painted on the walls, complete with blazing tiger-eyes. There were treasures everywhere: pressed flowers from the woods, rocks split open to reveal sparkling crystals, and mounted butterflies. And perhaps the most mysterious of all, the instruments with which John studied the electric fluid that he knew would change the world.

She remembered the day, years ago, when he introduced her to electric sparks, his eyes dancing as he proclaimed that he had mastered the techniques of handling them. He had told her, with a shy smile, that he was the universal man and God had chosen him to reveal important truths to all the world. Then, just as his understanding and powers of explanation were soaring to a peak, they suddenly collapsed and trickled into nothing. How distressed he'd been! "I had it straight," he'd cried as he ran both hands through his

21

tangled hair. "But now I've lost it all. What's plus turns out to be what's minus, and, Shua, I'm all mixed up." The trembling of his fingers frightened her as he picked imaginary lint from his black woolen jacket. "I can't get it right, Shua. I'm not good enough."

But now, full of confidence, he pointed to a bright new piece of apparatus. "I ordered it from London," he explained as he began to demonstrate what it could do. "Watch carefully." He cranked out sparks that crackled through the air—little ones at first, soon bigger, more impressive, noisier, until at last they sounded like gunshots.

"Marvelous, are they not?" He was intent on her reaction. "Exciting. Fascinating. Irresistible. But look now! See, as they get stronger, how like lightning they become. And lightning, Shua, can destroy."

She nodded and stepped back. She understood. She had come because she wanted Uncle John's advice, but now that he was giving it, she didn't want to listen.

Riding home, Bathsheba was more than ever at a loss. She always had believed that Uncle John, although generally considered daft, was wiser than anyone she knew. But wisdom did not help her now; there was something more profound at work. She almost hoped that fate would intervene, and Mr Spooner would not pay a call as he had promised. That way she would have no need to act, one way or another. But that wasn't what she wanted either. She wanted to take charge, but the trouble was, she did not know what path to follow.

Bathsheba was still with Uncle John in New Braintree when Joshua arrived at the Ruggles house in Hardwick carrying a bouquet of purple asters.

"Mrs Ruggles?" he asked of the striking woman who answered the door. He introduced himself. "Last night I met your daughter at the Danforth party. I brought her home, in fact, since she wasn't feeling well."

Sheba took her time to look him over. "That's news to me," she said, her eyebrows arched. She wasn't one to hold back her opinions and she was about to ask why he thought he had the right to escort her daughter anywhere when suddenly she softened. "You know," she said, "I think perhaps we have already met." She paused, trying to remember. "At Margaret Oliver's wedding? Yes, that's it. John Spooner is you brother, or a cousin maybe?"

"The groom was my brother."

Sheba smiled slightly. "Forgive me for not putting two and two together right away. There are so many Spooners hereabouts that the connection quite escaped me. Margaret's brother Daniel lives in Hardwick, you know, an apprentice in my husband's legal practice."

"I should have come to visit him. That way I might have met your daughter sooner."

"Well, she isn't here right now."

"Perhaps, then, you'd be so kind as to see that she gets these." Joshua handed her the asters. "This type is extremely rare. They grow wild in a sunny, sheltered place on my property in Brookfield. I find wild flowers especially lovely."

Sheba stepped back from the doorway. "Come in, you might as well." She led him to the parlor. "Lord knows where Bathsheba's gone or when she will be back. She's a bit of a wild flower herself."

As they chatted, Sheba took his measure. He's too elegant for these parts, she thought, too urbane to quite fit in. But he certainly was charming. Without seeming a bit obsequious, he complimented her on her choice of parlor furnishings, especially the gilt-framed mirror above the mantel. His comments were informed, and it was clear he knew a good piece when he saw one. He inquired about the Brigadier with just the right amount of deference.

"The Olivers speak highly of your brother John," she said. It wouldn't hurt to at least be civil.

Joshua seized the opening and launched into his credentials. His father, John Spooner Sr, had died two years ago. Born in Sheffield, England, he had moved to Boston early on, had become a merchant and amassed a modest fortune, a handsome share of which, Joshua implied, he had inherited. His mother, Elizabeth Wells, was descended through the Savages from Anne and William Hutchinson.

23

"Making my maternal lineage of interest, I'm sure you will agree," he added.

Sheba nodded. "You're trying to tell me you're a distant cousin of my husband's friend, the Lieutenant Governor." She smiled; it was easy to see through him. "Does your mother still live in Boston?" she asked.

"She died when I was very young." His expression darkened when he mentioned the stepmother who had brought him up.

Sheba cut through to something more important. "Do you practice one of the professions?"

Joshua took out his mermaid pipe, filled it, and tamped down the tobacco. "I'm a trader."

Judging from his clothes, she thought, he must be pretty good at it, or else he's dipping into his inheritance. "What kind of trading?"

"Tea, fabric, a little ivory, imported goods, that sort of thing. I have connections in India through London." He reached for the pipe tongs on the hearth. "May I?" Without waiting for an answer, he touched the tobacco with a hot coal and drew in. Sheba noticed the erotic carving on the meerschaum and was about to challenge him, but before she had a chance, he was saying, "Fact is, I'm a little new at this trading thing. Until recently, I've had the luxury of studying at the College in New Haven, mathematics and natural philosophy."

Sheba raised her eyebrows. From thinking to trading, how very odd. "Why did you leave Yale?"

"To take up my business. Theoretical inquiries are stimulating, but they won't keep a wife and family." He met Sheba's sharp look with a disarming smile. "I've taken too much of your time," he said. "Forgive me. But with your permission, I'll return."

She would rather he would not, but she understood her daughter well enough to know that forbidding him to come might lead Bathsheba to less acceptable alternatives.

Coming up the long driveway leading to her father's yellow house, Bathsheba met her mother on her way to meet the post rider. "You had a visitor while you were gone," Sheba announced. "A Mr

Spooner. He left some flowers—rare, late-blooming asters from his garden, or so he said. They're in the front hall on the table."

So Joshua had kept his word, and even brought some flowers! Bathsheba reddened and suppressed a smile.

"We had a little chat, Mr Spooner and I," Sheba went on. "I take it that he brought you home last night, very late. I was awake when you came in, but I thought you'd been with Nathan, and I wasn't bothered. I would have worried had I known what was really going on." Bathsheba stroked Bridie's mane, looking straight ahead. "I don't like this Mr Spooner," Sheba continued. "He's a charmer, I'll give him that, but there's something about him I don't trust."

That's Mama, making a quick judgment about someone she's just met.

Sheba flipped through her letters as if checking the addresses, then, with exaggerated slowness, put them in her pocket and looked up. "Mr Spooner asked for permission to come back."

"And you said...?"

"He'd come one way or another if he wanted to, no matter what anybody said." Sheba regarded her daughter critically. "You look worn out. Go get some rest."

Interviews with Mama were never easy, and, now that this one was finally at an end, Bathsheba sighed relief—a private sigh, not obvious enough to start her mother off again—and took Bridie to her stall. "Please take care of her," she said to the stable boy. Usually she fed and groomed her mare herself, but not this afternoon. Instead, she went directly to the house, gathered up the asters, and took them to her room.

As she idly rearranged the flowers to her better satisfaction, thoughts of Nathan kept encroaching. She told herself that it was nothing but a habit, thinking about him when she was alone. In her mind's eye, she could see him walking up the driveway, carrying two rabbits, swinging them by their hind legs in rhythm with his stride. He was always bringing presents to her mother. "Fresh caught for stew," she could almost hear him say.

Mr Spooner would never do a thing like that. Mr Spooner, likely, had never caught a rabbit in his life.

25

Chapter 5

Two days passed, uneasy days, and then, in the middle of a vivid thunderstorm, Mr Spooner appeared at the front door. He tipped his tricorn hat, and a little stream of water splashed down onto the granite step. "Are you going to invite me in?" he asked.

He looked daring and romantic, silhouetted for an instant against a flash of lightning. Bathsheba took his dripping wraps and hung them on the wall-pegs in the hall. Determined not to let him see her flustered like a child, she made a proper gesture toward the parlor. "The room is a bit damp and clammy, though," she said. "I'll fetch some kitchen coals, start a fire." Forgetting to invite him to sit down, she hurried off, relieved to get away, if only for a minute, in order to collect herself.

She scarcely noticed that he did not help her with the kindling and the logs, and when the fire was crackling, she took the chair by the love seat where he had settled. "No one else is home," she said. "So you must not stay too long."

"Don't look so prim." He laughed at her, and she reacted with a flare of anger. But it was immediately snuffed out when he withdrew from his pocket a parcel wrapped in a large handkerchief on which "J S" was embroidered on one corner. "For you," he said.

Bathsheba hesitated. It was the initialed handkerchief that gave her pause, for she well knew that in accepting it she would be encouraging Mr Spooner as a suitor, and she wasn't at all certain about that. She shook her head.

"Come on," he teased. "It won't bite. What are you worried about?" He placed the gift on the candle table, and studied her a moment. "I know what's troubling you. You've got Danforth on your mind. I can tell."

"No, you're wrong!" But he was indeed on target.

Joshua shrugged and nudged his present toward her, just a little. Slowly she reached out and took it. Then, startled by a clash of thunder, she almost dropped the gift. She untied the crimson bow with nervous fingers and found, to her astonishment, a treatise by someone named the Marquise du Chatelet. She looked up with questions in her eyes.

"I got it through my dealer in London," he told her. "The Marquise writes on scientific matters, and this is a translation and analysis of Newton's great *Principia*. I thought you might be interested."

Bathsheba glanced from Mr Spooner to the book and back again, then ran her fingers over the gold tooling on its dark blue leather cover. "I'm pleased," she said, still puzzled. But what an honor to have this man think of her this way! She opened the book and gave a little exclamation of surprise when she saw the text was all in French. No man, no one, had ever given her a gift like this.

"I'll help you translate," he assured her.

"Thank you, but I have no trouble reading French."

"Well then, I'll help you with the concepts. I know them well. I haven't read Madame du Chatelet's work as yet, and I am curious to see how Voltaire's mistress copes with Newton's views." He gave her a sidelong glance. "Voltaire wrote the preface, you will note, and I wonder just how much he influenced the rest." He smiled a conspiratorial smile. "And in what ways," he added and smiled again.

She knew a bit about Voltaire and his attacks on injustice and intolerance, and she had even managed to obtain and read a copy of *Candide*. How delicious that the famous Frenchman had a mistress, and more importantly, that Mr Spooner knew all about it, almost as if he were a friend of the Marquise.

As he leaned forward to inspect the book with her, a long gold chain fell from the folds of his white shirt, and its locket shimmered in the firelight. Distracted, Bathsheba could not focus on the pages she was turning. She heard Mr Spooner's words, but she was conscious only of the locket.

"Young ladies are usually gratified by novels," he was saying. "But something told me this would suit you better." He placed the locket back beneath his shirt.

"Thank you, but in truth, I'm very fond of novels."

Joshua's dark eyes flashed. The moment passed, but not before it occurred to her that he had seemed about to censure her remarks, even her thoughts, perhaps.

He straightened his cravat, smiling that smile that she did not understand. "It's time to go," he said. He bowed and kissed her hand. "I'll be back," he added. "Maybe tomorrow." He strode into the hall and took down his greatcoat from the peg.

Disconcerted by his abrupt decision to depart, she could think of nothing in return but a faint goodbye.

As he let himself out into the storm, a gust of wet wind swept through the hallway.

Three days went by, but Joshua did not come or even send a message. Maybe, Bathsheba thought, her mother had been right: he wasn't to be trusted. Maybe he had just been toying with her, a kind of sport for him.

On the fifth day, she made up her mind. She would not be trifled with. She would go to him and ask outright exactly how he stood. She had a right to know, and she needed to know now. "Come on, love," she said to Bridie as she took down the saddle. "Would you like a trip to Brookfield? We'll gallop half the way. That would please you, wouldn't it?"

The proprietor of Cooley's Tavern raised his eyebrows when she stepped up to the bar to ask directions to the Spooner house, but he remained polite. "Not far from here," he said, pointing in an easterly direction. "It's on the left, close to the road. You'll know it by the wide stone fence and high well curb."

Within minutes she was tethering Bridie to the hitching post beside the well and admiring the view that stretched for miles to the hills beyond. But for all her bravado, the clucking of the chickens in the yard seemed deafeningly loud, and a little sound at the front door was enough to make her jump.

"Good morning!" A pleasant-looking woman, maybe in her forties, was standing in the doorway. "Can I help you?"

Good Lord, Bathsheba thought. But after a moment's panic, her reason told her that the woman's homespun dress of rustic cut was not what the mistress of the house would wear. "I've come to see Mr Spooner," she said.

"He's not up yet, Miss. Though I expect he'll be about in just a little while. My name is Sarah Stratten and I do for him. Would you like to wait inside?"

Bathsheba's immediate reaction was to refuse the invitation and fib a little, saying she was merely stopping by to say hello on her way home from Worcester where she'd been visiting her sister Mary. But before she was able to say anything, she was following the woman.

Left alone, she glanced around the sitting room, from one curious object to another. In the corner was a harpsichord like one she'd seen in Worcester in the Chandler's parlor. On a shelf beside the fireplace was a small oriental statue made of teak inlaid with silver, an ancient bearded sage standing underneath a canopy of blossoms and carrying a lotus leaf. Seashells from exotic places were arranged in a shallow cut-glass dish. On a curly maple table was an open leather case lined with frayed red velvet, containing a pair of dueling pistols, each bearing the carved initial "S." Too old, Bathsheba thought, to have been wrought for Joshua, perhaps they'd been his father's.

She bent over to examine a handsome piece of scrimshaw depicting Lucifer in the act of ravishing a maiden. She wasn't in the habit of touching other people's things, but the piece intrigued her, and she picked it up. Absorbed in her examination of its explicit detail, she gasped when Joshua suddenly appeared.

He showed no surprise at seeing her, almost as if he'd been expecting her. "You find it interesting, I see," he said.

"I'm sorry." She replaced the object and stood waiting.

He was wearing an oriental banyan made of rich brown silk, its pink lining exposed on its collar and rolled cuffs. His waistcoat was unbuttoned to the waist, his white linen shirt open at the throat, revealing his gold chain.

He went over to his porcelain rum dispenser, poured himself a drink and tipped the glass in her direction. She shook her head. "Some tea, then," he said, and called to Mrs Stratten without shifting his gaze from Bathsheba, not for a moment. She felt impaled and she could not think of anything to say. He made no attempt to fill the gap, and not until Mrs Stratten had put down the tea tray and gone back to the kitchen did Bathsheba speak.

"You may deem it foolish," she began. "But I had to see you."

"I'm glad." He crossed his arms and stroked his silken sleeves. "And you had no trouble finding me? No, of course not. You're a clever girl."

Bathsheba poured her tea from cup to saucer. "But not an easy girl," she said, "despite what must have been your original impression." Embarrassed by her memories, she glanced away and did not see Joshua's amused expression. "You haven't been to see me in five days, although you promised you'd come daily."

Joshua closed his eyes and slowly shook his head from side to side, seemingly incredulous at being so misunderstood.

Bathsheba pushed ahead. "Your manner leads me to believe you regard me as a mere pastime. If I'm nothing to you but a toy, I insist we stop."

Joshua put up both hands, palms facing her in a manner indicating that he didn't want to hear another word. "My dear," he soothed. "Don't upset yourself. I couldn't come to see you because I was away. You must learn to accept such things. I often need to go away on business." He fingered his gold chain, drew out his locket and set it spinning. "Don't harbor any foolish notions," he said. "I want you to understand that this courtship means everything to me. I mean to marry you. That's what I've had in mind from the moment I found you in Danforth's garden."

Bathsheba's eyes grew wide. Was she hearing him correctly?

He replaced the locket, then picked up his glass and swirled its contents. "You asked, so there it is, a proposal as serious as anything

I've ever done." He paused and sat watching her. "Judging from your look," he said, "I think I've taken you aback."

She stared at him.

"Of course, I don't expect an answer right away. This will be our little secret for awhile."

Thank God, Bathsheba thought. Thank God for the protocol about such matters. A well-bred girl would never even think of accepting the first proposal a man made. Every woman needed time. She used to think that rule of social etiquette was silly, but now she understood its usefulness. More importantly, now at least she was convinced he wasn't playing games. She stood up and took his hand and brought him to her side. Parting his shirt beneath his banyan, she took out his locket and pressed it hard against her lips.

Chapter 6

"He's home!" the stable boy called in from the kitchen door. "Rode all night, but insists on tending to Midnight himself. He's out there now."

Bathsheba put down her cup of morning coffee and grabbed her shawl. She ran past the barn and the long line of stables to the large stall reserved for the Brigadier's black stallion. "Papa! At last!" How good to see him! How tired he looks. "Welcome home," she said, rushing to embrace him, bursting to tell him what had happened to her while he was away, but she held back. She could see that he was out of sorts, exhausted.

He poured a bucket of fresh water into the horse's trough. "I walked out," he said. "Damned nonsense, petitioning London, illegally at that. I told them so. Wrong-headed. An upstart representing Delaware went so far as to challenge me to a duel." He snorted his disdain. Although elected the chairman of the Congress, he had not conformed. "That chairman deal was a political maneuver, to shut me up, keep me from making speeches from the floor. But they couldn't stop me from refusing to sign their damned petitions." He also refused to give his reasons. "Should have been obvious. I've never hid my views from anyone. So I walked out. Mad as hell!"

"Yes." Bathsheba was no stranger to her father's temper.

"But that was a damned fool thing to do." He looked a little sheepish. "I was a God damned fool!"

No doubt. The Whig politicians would play the incident against him, make political hay with it.

"Where's your mother?" he asked, as they started toward the house.

"In Worcester, visiting Mary and her family."

"Just as well, for a while at least."

"Gives you time to calm down a bit?" Bathsheba was the only child of his brood of seven who would dare make a remark like that.

"You're your mother's daughter," the Brigadier said, and smiled.

The Brigadier's enemies demanded that the Speaker of the House reprimand him publicly before his peers, and then they voted to deny his request to enter the reasons for his actions in the Assembly Record Book. Never mind; he would publish his defense in the *Boston Post-Boy*. That way, it would reach a wider audience anyway.

And in the end, Bathsheba thought, the rebels will be proven wrong. Papa will wind up a hero again, praised for his foresight and his understanding of Parliamentary law and politics. She agreed with his unbending attitude, his certainty that the rebels, left unchecked, would bring disaster to the colony. She was glad that, at least so far, most of Hardwick's voters deplored the turmoil in Boston, with the port closed and business at a standstill in defiance of the Stamp Act, the buildings along King Street all draped in black. "But we'll have no mourning here in Hardwick," the Brigadier announced, and he told sister Martha and John Tufts to go ahead with wedding plans.

The banns were published on the eleventh of November, and the Brigadier sent Moses, his right-hand man, to read out invitations for a reception to be held the day following the nuptials. He included on his guest list everyone he knew in Hardwick, even a political enemy or two, as well as friends from as far away as Boston.

For a fortnight, the Ruggles house was in a flurry. Sheba oversaw a general housecleaning, made sure that the family silver gleamed, and told cook to lay in special provisions for the feast. To help sister Elizabeth and the seamstress make new gowns for everyone, Mary came from Worcester, bringing her husband, Dr Green, and their three sons, all less than five years old. "What nuisances," Bathsheba said. But she adored them.

Romance was on everybody's mind, and Bathsheba beamed when Joshua promised to ask her father soon, in a proper manner, for her hand. "Sometime after Martha's wedding," he said. "We mustn't shift attention from her special day." How marvelously considerate he is, Bathsheba thought.

Nathan came by with a present, a ham that he had cured himself. He sought out Bathsheba and found her in the stable tending Bridie. "For the reception," he said somewhat stiffly. "No one seems to be around, so I left it in the kitchen. Would you tell Martha for me, please."

Bathsheba could think of nothing reasonable to say. How awkward, how different from how it used to be. He knew that she was seeing Joshua, everyone in Hardwick knew. She wondered if she should ask after Mary Jackson, but she couldn't bring herself to that. She was tongue-tied, and Nathan just stood there, distant, looking at her in a peculiar way.

With only the immediate family present, the Brigadier, splendid in his crimson judge's robe, led John and Martha through their marriage vows before the fire in the best parlor. Then he took John's hand and placed it over Martha's. "I vouchsafe her to your care," he said, and motioned Timothy, as his eldest son, to fill the glasses with champagne.

The sun was shining brightly the next afternoon, as beribboned coaches started to arrive—the Olivers from Middleborough, the Leonards from Norton, the Murrays from Rutland, and the Chandlers from Worcester. The Boston people got there late, dazzling everybody with their finery, as Sheba said they meant to do. The ladies wore rich silks and satins with long trains, their hair puffed, powdered, and rolled high on their heads. "I'm quite worn out," one matron complained to Sheba. "I sat up all night in order that my hairdresser's handiwork might not be disarranged."

Sheba's smile wasn't sympathetic.

In contrast with this *haute monde* style, Bathsheba's lustrous black hair was arranged in a simple twist interwoven with a strand of tiny pearls, a gift from Grandmother Bourne. Her gown of yellow silk was décolleté and short, well above her ankles, and unadorned except for an embroidered hem. Radiant, she moved from guest to guest, greeting them and introducing Joshua. He was as elegant as any man from Boston, his forest-green velvet coat set off with white lace ruffles at the neck and sleeves. "You're clearly making an impression," she whispered, her pride and pleasure glowing.

And yet, throughout the evening, little things kept reminding her of Nathan—the chiming of the tall clock, which he once had said must be the finest of its kind in Worcester County; the greens from the deer park, which in other years he'd helped gather for family parties. She had been relieved when he sent formal regrets, saying he would be in Boston. Yet, despite his absence, he seemed to be everywhere in her father's house tonight.

She had just finished a contredanse with Joshua when Judge Oliver's son William touched her elbow. "The musicians are promising a reel," he said. "Will you honor me?" She could sense Joshua's disapproval, but she could not refuse. William was a guest, and to decline would be ill-mannered. Besides, she knew from past experience that he was a jolly partner, and she soon was laughing as they moved together down between the rows of dancers. Gardner Chandler claimed her next, then William was back again. Her head was spinning with the pleasure of it all—until she noticed Joshua watching her.

Supper was served at midnight: venison, a salad made from rabbit breast, and roast pig from the barbecue outside. Silver bowls were filled with fruit kept fresh in the root cellar since harvest. The sillabub flowed freely, and the bride and groom were toasted many times, along with Queen Charlotte and King George. Martha cut the cake, and Bathshcba helped wrap small slices in squares of multicolored silk for the young unmarried women to take home—to ensure a happy marriage in the future, it was said. Bathsheba placed her portion in an enameled box on the sideboard, intending to take it to her room later in the evening.

At last the musicians packed up their instruments, and the guests began to leave. Slowly the house quieted. Sheba and the Brigadier were already sleeping. The newlyweds went up to Martha's chamber, and others in the family retired one by one until finally Bathsheba was alone with Joshua.

"I want us to get married soon," he said abruptly. "As soon as possible."

"I'd like that, too," she said. "In the spring? Or is that *too* soon?"

"Not soon enough. I'm going to ask your father for your hand tomorrow. I hope we'll post the banns within a fortnight."

A fortnight!

"You look upset," he said.

She accepted his embrace and helped him with his greatcoat.

Before snuffing out the candles, she stepped over to the sideboard to retrieve her morsel of the wedding cake. But it wasn't there, it wasn't anywhere. Unduly troubled by her loss, she went to bed but could not sleep. Thoughts of Nathan kept creeping through her mind. In the quiet of the night, she missed him, and, for the first time, she was shocked at how fast her life had changed, now to be married to Joshua within weeks! For what seemed like hours, she tried lying first this way, then that, until finally her thoughts began to blur, and a dream of happiness took over—a dream of Nathan.

Chapter 7

Joshua stood waiting, thinking that the Brigadier's study, though small, was overwhelming, with its paneled mahogany walls and an air of English authority. The large mahogany desk that almost filled the room was covered with legal-looking documents, and a sword, crossed over its sheath, was hanging on the wall behind it. The Brigadier's teakwood cane with the carved ivory handle was propped against his chair. Legal tomes crowded the untidy bookshelves that lined one of the walls, and a bear rug, complete with head and gaping jaws, was spread out on the floor before the fire.

Joshua fussed with his wrist lace, then reached into his pocket to fondle his meerschaum. He must not fail to win the Brigadier's approval. He must secure Bathsheba while she was still brimming with illusions. Above all, he must not risk the chance that someone else—an Oliver or a Chandler—might come along and capture her attention. Or worse, that she might drift back to that bumpkin, Nathan Danforth.

At the sound of approaching footsteps, he tensed. The Brigadier paused a moment in the doorway, filling it and dominating the small room. Joshua was struck for the first time by the impressive stature of the man, six feet tall, still handsome in his mid-fifties, with a strong commanding face. Judging by his apparel, Joshua concluded he had come directly from the stables, and he had the uneasy feeling that he himself was almost ridiculously overdressed for the occasion.

The Brigadier shook his hand, sat down, and motioned that Joshua should do the same. "Of course, I know why you've asked to see me," he said.

"Yes. Well, sir, I've made no secret of my intentions toward your daughter."

"And just why do you think I should agree to such a marriage?"

Joshua hesitated, caught off guard. Surely, he thought, the man already knows I come from a good family.

"Yes, yes," the Brigadier said, as if reading Joshua's mind. "I knew your father, not well, but he was prominent enough in Boston for all of us around the town to at least know *of* him. And, although you probably do not recall, my wife and I attended the reception after Margaret Oliver's marriage to your brother John."

"I recall only vaguely, sir. It was a large affair and several years ago." Damn John, Joshua thought. In the end, though, he would get even. Bathsheba was more beautiful than Margaret and Brigadier General Ruggles was as well known and as rich as Margaret's father. Of course, at the moment, both of these prominent Loyalists were in trouble, but the recent unpleasantness, violent as some of it had been, surely would blow over soon. And when the dust settled, Joshua Spooner would be a member of a family favored by the Crown.

"I hold the Olivers in high regard," the Brigadier was saying. "And from time to time I've heard them speak well of your family."

Joshua relaxed a little. He was banking on the relationship between the Spooners and Olivers to help advance his suit. He was certain the Brigadier would object to the marriage of any of his daughters to a man opposed to Loyalists. Of course, in point of fact, he himself paid little mind to politics, but for the purposes at hand, it was good to be seen on the right side. He took out his pipe. "Do you mind, sir?" he asked.

"Yes."

A mistake, Joshua thought. He must be careful. Anything might constitute a setback.

"Tell me, why did you move from Boston?"

Joshua was prepared for this. "I like country life, sir, just as you do. I'm no lover of the competition that is rife among the Boston merchants, and I'm doing well as a trader here, with a little time left over for philosophical ponderings."

"I see. I know of your inheritance," the Brigadier continued. "A handsome enough sum, £4,000. May I ask what you plan to do with it?"

"I have already helped Margaret Oliver's cousins with a loan of £1,000. I consider it an investment."

"As well you might," the Brigadier allowed. "The security the Olivers gave you is quite significant. One half their silting mills in Middleborough isn't bad."

My God, this man knows everything. Small wonder he has the reputation of being a hard man to deal with.

"And can I be sure you are sincere in your affection for my daughter?"

"I could not be more so. I could not wish for anyone more suited to my desires." That was true, as far as it went. Enough said; it would be madness to even hint at the nature of his erotic needs.

The Brigadier turned to other, less basic aspects of the union, Joshua's personal interests, and where he planned to settle down for good. Finally he stood up. "Come back tomorrow for my answer."

"Yes," Sheba said, as she sat down in the chair Joshua had occupied an hour or so earlier. "I can understand why you've decided to give him your consent. After all, I allowed him to come here in the first place, day after day while you were away, even though the more I got to know him, the more uneasy I became."

"Uneasy? Why?"

"He's clever, of course," Sheba conceded. "He seems like the most generous, most gifted person in the world. He figures out what people's interests are and then plays on them. Take you, for example, he's got you pegged. You've been flattered half to death by his feigned curiosity about your methods of cross-pollinating different kinds of fruits."

"What do you mean, 'feigned'?"

"I doubt he really cares a whit, or even listens to your explanations. When I questioned him about the orchards on his place, he let slip that he didn't have a single apple tree, much less an orchard."

"If you felt so strongly all along, why in the name of God did you not call a halt? I've never known you to hold back."

"What good would it have done, with him bewitching everybody in the family? Furthermore—you know her as well as I do—one word from me and Bathsheba would have reared up in revolt."

The Brigadier took on his judicial look. "For my part, I see Spooner as quite appropriate," he said. "He has some money and good sense in handling it. He's well-bred and educated, at least to some degree. It's also of some importance, I think you will agree, that he seems to be as much in love with Shua as she is with him."

With a wave of her hand Sheba dismissed such nonsense. "She could wait six months at least," she said. "That might be enough time for something to happen that would remove the scales from her eyes."

"On the contrary, I've given this considerable thought, and I'm all for going right ahead. Bathshua's welfare is my overriding concern." He spoke with deep conviction. "It was clear to me from my observations at the Congress in New York that the colonies are beginning to take a united stand—and that, my dear, does not augur well. These are unsettled times, and I'd like to see Shua married soon, and to someone with no political enemies. I'm convinced that Spooner's ties are in the right camp, although, in my judgment, he's basically indifferent—politically, I mean. That's advantageous; neither side will consider him an enemy. Shua will be safe with him should the violence pick up, which I have little doubt it will."

"Safe!" Sheba stood up, defiant. She indicated the jumble of legal books and papers on his desk. "You may understand the subtleties of litigation, but not the problems that a woman faces." Her own widow's dower after her first husband's death had given her considerable leverage, and, despite the fact that she trusted the Brigadier as much as any man, she had insisted on a contract that gave her certain rights, especially when it came to managing her money. But their daughter wasn't quite in that position.

"Shua needs a generous man, a man of freer, larger stature than this Spooner; she needs a giant of a man." Sheba paused, her expression softened by her memories. The Brigadier's eyes caught hers and a warm spark passed between them.

Sheba became grave and less belligerent. "He drinks too much, which apparently you haven't noticed—not exactly surprising what with all the political upheaval that is troubling you. But even more than that, there's something intangible that I don't trust about the man." She was serious as death. "I can't exactly put my finger on it."

The Brigadier threw up his hands. "Good God! You're the last woman on earth I would ever have expected to take to soothsaying. Joshua's inheritance and prospects and political neutrality are what matter, not some mysterious quirk you fancy that you see in him!"

Defeated but far from humbled, she turned to leave the room. "No use trying to reason with a man like you," she said before she closed the door.

Sheba failed not only to bring the Brigadier around, but also to convince her daughter to postpone the wedding until spring. Even her most pragmatic argument fell short. "You can't have a big reception in the dead of winter when traveling is so bad. We couldn't count on anybody coming."

Bathsheba shot back that Joshua didn't want a party anyway, and she didn't either, anymore, although she admitted that not so long ago she had dreamed of a grand reception, equal to Martha's or even grander. "We want a simple affair," she insisted. "Just our immediate family and Uncle John. Joshua doesn't even want his brothers to attend."

"That in itself should tell you something." But Sheba knew her cause was lost.

On January 8, 1766, the banns were published, and at noon ten days later, as dark snow clouds gathered, Bathsheba became Joshua Spooner's wife. She looked paler than usual as she stood at his side before her father and vowed to honor and obey her husband until death.

Gravely, she kissed each member of her family, then went to the stables to say goodbye to Bridie and make arrangements for Moses to bring the mare to Brookfield the next day. When at last she was ready, she went outside with Uncle John to wait for Joshua to come by with his sleigh. "I hope you know," John said, "that no matter what I've indicated in the past, I wish you nothing but the best."

"I know. We'll invite you for a visit as soon as we get settled. I'm..." Her voice trailed off as she caught sight of Nathan striding up the long, snow-covered drive.

He was facing her by now, his expression solemn, although he smiled. "I've come to say goodbye and wish you happiness," he said. "We may not see each other often in the future, but I won't forget the good times we've had together."

Unforgettable good times. "I'll miss you," Bathsheba said as she reached out and took his hand. He held it for a moment, then turned to go. As she watched him walk back down the drive, a feeling of emptiness came over her. But she had no time to dwell on it, for at that moment Joshua's sleigh appeared, and her life with him began.

Chapter 8

"I'm cold." Bathsheba pulled the bear rug closer. "We should have stayed the night."

The only response she received was the rhythmic clip-clop of the horse's hooves and the zing of runners gliding over snow.

"Mama wished it." She pictured John and sister Martha on their wedding night, warm by the fire in Martha's room. "We should have stayed at least one night."

Dusk was thick with snowflakes by the time they drew up to Joshua's barn. "Take care of the horse," he instructed Jesse. "And bring Mrs Spooner's trunk inside." He helped her from the sleigh. "Go on in," he said. "I'll be a minute more."

Mrs Stratten was waiting at the kitchen door, concern flickering in her eyes. "Cold night, too cold for travel." She led Bathsheba to the settle and filled the teapot from the kettle on the trivet.

Bathsheba warmed her hands. "Yes, too cold," she said. "I think the trip has made Mr Spooner out of sorts."

"Aye, ma'am. Don't think on it."

"No." She considered her shadowy surroundings. "I've never seen a fireplace so massive," she said. The hearth was wide; a powder horn and musket hung on the oaken lintel. In addition to the usual brick oven and iron pot, there were two roasting ovens and an iron spider. An unusual brick arch curved overhead.

"It supports the hearth in the master's chamber up above," Mrs Stratten explained. "Now tell me, ma'am, about the wedding." She took from the dresser a hand painted Dresden cup and its matching saucer. "Cream? Do you like it sweetened too?"

43

Bathsheba reached for the fragrant beverage, smiling thanks. "The wedding was a quiet affair, just as we wished. My father led us through our vows. He's a judge, you know."

"Aye, everybody knows. 'Tis good that way, your father doing that for you." She fed the fire another log. "I must go now, ma'am. The snow, you know, and I have a long walk home. I've laid out cold supper in the sitting room for you and Mr Spooner, a fire too."

Bathsheba followed Joshua from the kitchen and sat quietly while he warmed himself and improved his temper with a glass of rum. She recalled her visit not so long ago when she sat where she was sitting now and he had assured her of his intentions. Now she was his wife, and he was offering her a drink. "Have a little. It's relaxing, smoothes the way."

She shook her head. The brightness in his eyes and the way he smiled told her that the time was near. She shivered, although she was no longer cold, but her frank desire soon overcame her uncertainty and she reached out to him.

He brought her down before the fire. "My prize," he said, and with practiced skill began to take possession. Eagerly, she gave herself, completely.

Afterwards, full of tenderness, she murmured her devotion.

He took out his mermaid pipe. "You're good," he said. His smile, as always, puzzled her—so cryptic, dark. He nodded to himself. "Excellent."

Beneath the surface of her mind, there flickered the impression that his words, his tone of voice, his expression, all suggested that she was to him like a highly satisfactory piece of merchandise, newly acquired and worth the price. She shook away the thought.

He sat down to Mrs Stratten's fresh made bread, cold roast with mustard, and a mix of beans. Bathsheba recoiled as he fell upon his food and washed it down with rum. He took another helping and motioned her to join him.

"No. I have no appetite, not any more." His features hardened. He evidently was interpreting her remark to mean something other than what she had intended, and, as she watched his anger kindle, she suddenly felt exhausted, no longer interested in trying to please him, in trying to explain. She took the candle from the stand. "Goodnight." She paused before she turned into the shadows and started up the steep, dark stairs. But he made no move to follow her.

There was no fire in Joshua's chamber, and a stale odor tinged the frigid air. She placed her candle on the windowsill and wrapped herself in the linsey-woolsey coverlet. Huddling there, watching the falling snow by candlelight, she could hear tortured strains from Joshua's harpsichord, coming from the room below. She began to weep.

Chapter 9

She sat alone in the chamber she had been sharing with her husband
for almost five months. It was much too hot for May, and for a
moment she considered opening the window, but she rejected the
idea. Closed, it shut out the noise from the celebration down the road
in Mr Hinckley's field. Brookfield, like every town throughout the
province, was using news of Repeal of the Stamp Act—which had
taken weeks to cross the ocean—as an excuse for a grand holiday.
Bathsheba, however, had no intention of joining the merrymakers. In
their inevitable speeches, the town fathers would glorify the Stamp
Act Congress that had brought her father down. They would take the
opportunity to publicly discredit him, make him out a traitor, and she,
his daughter, refused to listen, take any part.

Mrs Stratten had asked to be excused after finishing the morning
chores. "I'd like to join the festivities a little, ma'am. It's not often we
have a chance like this."

Yes, of course, enjoy yourself. Mrs Stratten never got a holiday,
and Bathsheba was glad that Joshua was not around to insist that she
put in a full day's work before slacking off. That's the way he'd put
it—"slacking off."

She was getting used to his frequent absences, all but welcoming
them. Not that she would ever be able to accept his secrecy, never
telling her where he was going, or why. She sometimes wondered if
he had a mistress, it certainly was possible; she well knew how
seductive he could be, consumed by lust. But maybe she was
expecting too much of marriage, maybe every couple goes through
something like this, maybe it should simply be endured, like pain in
childbirth. She could, of course, compare notes with sister Martha,

settled with her own new husband across town. On the other hand, to indicate in any way that she was unhappy and confused might easily be seen to mean that she was flawed in her duties as a wife—or worse, that maybe she had made a big mistake. No, best not to share with Martha.

She thought about her life in Hardwick, so unlike here. There relationships were open, frank, and unrestrained. Her mother ran her household without interference from her father, and although her parents often disagreed and sometimes quarreled—often fiercely— there was never the tight, uneasy feeling that pervaded Joshua's house, the lack of compromise. Joshua was maddening. He dismissed out of hand her ideas about everything from redecorating the dark sitting room to interpreting the meaning of a passage in a book. Moreover, he hugged his possessions like a little boy. Everything belonged to him and him alone. He declared off limits the treasures she so admired. "Don't touch that ivory carving, please. I wouldn't want to be obliged to hold you responsible if anything should happen." Or, "Mrs Stratten will take care of dusting in the sitting room. She knows how to handle things." Joshua, the husband, Bathsheba was discovering, was very different from Joshua, the suitor. She wanted to go home.

The din was rising from the growing crowd next door, and the heat was getting worse. Bathsheba loosened the ribbon at her throat and let her shift fall lower on her shoulders. She rose and felt her way down the steep front stairs, lit only by three bull's-eye windows over the front door. When she opened it, blinding light assaulted her, and she stepped back. Then, as her eyes became accustomed, she saw two strangers laughing and relaxing on the stone fence by the road. They were young and bearded, with long, tangled hair and clothes of coarse homespun. Travelers, she thought, and, with a need to be with someone, she called out to them. "Hello! Can I help you?"

They turned, surprised. "No thank you, ma'am," the taller one replied. "Not unless you can do something about this heat!"

"You're welcome to some fresh water, over there." Bathsheba pointed to the well.

They laughed. "No thanks. We're not wanting water." He winked and held up his worn leather pocket flask. "Would you like a little, ma'am?"

Bathsheba ventured closer. "Where are you folks headed, anyway?" At the thought of Joshua's reaction should he find her with these men, she withdrew a little—but only for a moment.

"Just to Worcester, ma'am." The stranger's voice was gravelly, a yeoman's voice. "Not far now. You by any chance familiar with that town?"

"A little. My sister lives there with her family." Emboldened, Bathsheba gathered up her skirts and ran to them, feeling adventurous, even a bit flirtatious. "How come you fellows aren't out there celebrating?"

"What's to celebrate? The Stamp Act never mattered much to us. We've not been dealing a whole lot with items needing paper, ma'am. We got no family, and no bills. Fact is, we can't neither of us cipher, nor can write." He cupped his hands around his mouth and leaned in her direction. "Anyway," he added, sotto voce, "you needn't go telling anyone, but even if we had a lot of cash, we'd steer our way around the Act one way or another." He grinned and beckoned her to join them.

All of Brookfield was at Hinkley's, and nobody would notice. Anyway, what did it matter? She accepted a taste of the travelers' wine—pretty bad, like vinegar. She listened to their tales of adventure on the road.

"Maybe you should come along," teased the shorter fellow with a wink. "We could show you one hell of a good time, excusing the expression, ma'am." He laughed. "Just a joke." He fished through his big pockets, pulled out a filthy handkerchief, inspected it, replaced it, and finally located his harmonica. He began to play "Whiskey in a Jar," and they all began to sing. An hour slipped by, and soon the sparks from Hinckley's bonfire could be seen against the evening sky. "We'd best be on our way," the tall man said. "We need to find a barn or field to spend the night. And filch a chicken, maybe, for our supper."

Should I ask them in to share a meal? She almost did, but they were already off, arms linked, singing. The wine had left her hazy. She wandered over to the well and gazed at the reflection of the half-moon in the dark water down below. She was glad the travelers had stopped by. They were without refinement, and their conversation, although witty, had no substance. But they were easy, and they treated her as if she mattered. Like Nathan used to do. In her dreamy, detached state, on this warm, fragrant evening, she longed for days that were forever gone. She longed for Nathan.

Chapter 10

1768

Cooley's Tavern was abuzz. The smell of stale beer, intensified by July heat, stirred memories of the Newcomb Inn in Sandwich, Sheba's inheritance from her first husband. Bathsheba had loved the smell of beer when she was little; it meant singing in the tap room, or her father setting up a game of quoits for travelers stopping by on their way to destinations on Cape Cod. It meant good will and entertainment, as now, with fiddle-music drifting from the Hinckley's party in Cooley's second story ball room—a party to which the Spooners had not been invited. Next door neighbors, but not invited.

"Your fault," Joshua said, contemplating his wife as he sipped his rum. Things had not worked out. Oh, she was still beautiful, more beautiful than when he'd married her. She had blossomed during her first pregnancy, and motherhood added a subtle glow. Men always glanced at her approvingly, ignoring their wives' gossip. The women held sway, however; Bathsheba and her Loyalist views were not welcome in their homes, and, guilty by association, Joshua wasn't either. His eyes narrowed with annoyance: his wife had become a serious detriment.

He had misjudged—terribly. The disagreements between the colonies and the mother country had not blown over as he had so confidently expected, and, during the past three years, his father-in-law's reputation had gone steadily down hill. Ever since the Stamp Act Congress, the Brigadier had repeatedly been on the wrong side, as just recently, when his was the single vote in the legislature against non-importation of British goods. And there was that debacle when he led a House minority of 17 who obeyed the order from the King to rescind an inflammatory letter widely circulated by Sam Adams. Of course, the "glorious ninety-two" who stuck with Adams, denouncing the Townshend Acts as "taxation without representation," were heralded as heroes. But Tim Ruggles was decried, and Joshua Spooner found himself married to the daughter of a hated Tory.

"Martha's always late," he said.

"Don't get testy. Remember, she invited us here to celebrate her birthday." It was a wonder that Joshua had agreed to come. They almost never went anywhere together anymore, which, no doubt, was just as well, he no longer was good company, not for Bathsheba, anyway. Of course, with others, he was still a charmer. Oh yes! He was the gentleman who dressed like a Bostonian, a sophisticated man who traded with merchants as far away as London and gave discounts on religious books from England to half the ministers in Worcester County. But with her he was another person, taking pleasure in a twisted way from treating her like an errant, stupid child.

Bathsheba caught sight of Martha and John Tufts silhouetted against the afternoon as they came through the tavern door. "At least it's cooler here inside," John said as Bathsheba rose to greet them.

The women fell to talking about their children—Bathsheba's Elizabeth and Martha's Mary. The cousins, both in the middle of their second year, were already frequent playmates. "I want them to be friends forever," Bathsheba said.

After ordering sillibub all round, John turned to Joshua. "I've something to show you." Not heeding Martha's expression of alarm in her attempt to warn him, he took from the pocket of his waistcoat a folded broadsheet and handed it to Joshua. A smile curled Spooner's lips as he studied the cartoon, and he gave a little snort of appreciation.

Bathsheba snatched the paper, and her face contorted as she took its meaning. "A Warm Place—Hell!" Seventeen rescinders marching into the maw of hell, one devil howling, "A fine hawl, by Jove," and another, pointing to the leader, urging "Push on, Tim."

Joshua was laughing, whispering to John. "Serves the old buzzard right."

Bathsheba crushed the offensive piece and hurled it at her husband. "Damn Paul Revere and his scurrilous cartoons! Damn Sam Adams and his pack of Patriots!" She damned Joshua beneath her breath, pushed back her chair, and turned to Martha. "I'm sorry to spoil your party."

Every eye in the tavern followed her as she walked, head high, superior, past the other patrons, out from the shadows of the taproom into the heat.

Joshua sat alone. John and Martha had excused themselves, embarrassed, apologizing for Bathsheba, saying that at heart, really, she meant well. "It's all right," they said.

All right?! Joshua brooded. It was preposterous, her raving over a cartoon, and a good one, too—witty, to the point. She's obsessed with her father. She's crazy, making enemies for me.

He was getting drunk, his mind close to the edge. No matter, his head would clear, and he would figure out some way to make her pay. He would think of something. He called to Cooley for some bread and cheese. "And black coffee, hear."

She was sitting on the floor of the sitting room, arranging wooden blocks into a tower for her little girl. Nearby a golden kitten chased her tail. Bathsheba heard him coming and looked up to see his face clouded over in a way she was beginning to dread. He was fingering his mermaid pipe. "A beautiful domestic scene," he said.

"I'm sorry. I should not have done it." She truly wanted to smooth things over, but then she immediately spoiled her own intentions: "You provoked it."

Always the last word! He towered over her, his silence full of malice. The atmosphere around him bristled as he turned away and slammed the door.

She picked up Elizabeth and stood at the window watching him stride down the road, his back rigid with defiance. She had done it again, made a mess of things. She should at least have swallowed that last remark, but she couldn't seem to help herself. She felt desperate.

She left Elizabeth with Mrs Stratten and went to Bridie. Once on the open road, she urged the mare to a canter, then a gallop, her thoughts pounding. Was her marriage hopeless? Was she to blame? Maybe it was she who was destroying it. Just yesterday Joshua had been nice to her, almost the man she once had thought so handsome and distinguished. His caress could still excite her, and she often yearned for it, yet she could never trust it. Her thoughts careened as she rushed on, almost as far as Worcester, until at last she slowed Bridie and turned back.

Evening came, cooler. She bathed Elizabeth and took her to her crib. She picked up her embroidery and started working on the collar of a shirt for Joshua. But the light was getting dim and her eyes refused. She put on the imported robe her father had given her the night before she married, she let down her braids and brushed her hair. For a tangle of reasons she did not understand, she wanted to look beautiful when Joshua returned. The thought kept persisting in the shadows of her mind that, if she were clever enough, she could somehow turn things around, take charge, and recapture the suitor who had won her. What special thing, she pondered, could make a difference? She waited, expectant, but Joshua did not come home.

"Would you like a party for your birthday?" she asked a few days later.

"Who would come? No one but your family, and not many of them."

He was right. Nobody would come. She felt sorry for him. She must think of something else, more intimate and private. His favorite meal, with wine? But she never could be sure he would be home, and he hated to be asked about his plans. A vest, perhaps, handsomely embroidered. She excelled at things like that, and he loved elegant apparel. Yes, that was it.

She began to filch from the household money, a little every week, so when the peddler made his rounds again, she could choose from fabrics in his wagon. A swath of dark blue velvet caught her eye.

She fashioned a pattern from his favorite garment, and cut and stitched when Joshua was away. She sketched a design that included his initials and, despite frequent bouts with nausea—pregnant again, she was sure—she managed to copy her invention in scarlet, gold, and silver threads. Mrs Stratten pronounced the vest a masterpiece. "Law, ma'am, it's a marvel, fit for the King," she said.

Bathsheba wrapped her present in paper on which she'd painted water-color asters, purple, like those Joshua had given her so long ago. She placed her gift on the candle table by his favorite chair, certain it would give him pleasure.

It grew late. Maybe, she thought, he won't come home tonight. That happened so often now, without any warning. But not tonight, please, not tonight.

The tall clock chimed twice. Elizabeth, sleeping on a cot beside the fire, woke and began to cry. "Hush," Bathsheba said, drying her own tears.

Then she heard him, entering heavily through the kitchen door. He sat down stiffly, saw the gift, and looked up at her. She nodded yes, it was for him. He reached for it and tore away the paper, not noticing the asters. "What's this?" He unfolded the garment and held it up. "Just when do you think I'll have occasion any more to wear a thing like this?" He tossed it toward her, but his aim was poor, and the garment fell inside the hearth. She jumped up and reached to save it, but too late. In anguish, she turned to him, only to meet his twisted smile.

As she watched the garment shrivel in the flames, she felt overwhelmed by hopelessness—abandoned, totally alone. He had never loved her. He never would.

Chapter 11

October, 1768

Great commotion and no little indignation accompanied the arrival of the British Regulars, muskets loaded and ready, marching down King Street. They were far from welcome, and the Select Men expressed the people's outrage by refusing to provide them quarters. The soldiers could spend the winter freezing in the streets, for all the Bostonians cared. Governor Bernard finally stepped in and offered Faneuil Hall and the Town House—to the great disruption of the market place and inconvenience of the government officials. This clearly would not do as a permanent solution, and General Gage journeyed from his New York headquarters to sort out the problem. Meanwhile, Bernard designated another government-owned building, which—he hadn't seemed to notice—was already home to a flock of indigents who insisted on their squatters' rights. Moreover, the Sons of Liberty promptly managed to fill up any remaining space by transferring people from the workhouse. Something of a circus followed. The sheriff, determined to oust the illegal occupants, entered through a window and got himself locked in. There he remained, jammed in with Boston's most impoverished dirty, smelly, ragged citizens, until the British soldiers rescued him, cleared out the building, and then moved in themselves.

With unwelcome Redcoats swarming all over town, Sam Adams began to publish his *Journal of Annoyances*, anonymous accounts which he distributed throughout the Colonies. These gems of propaganda described the horrors suffered by beleaguered inhabitants trying to survive under military rule—wanton attacks, rapes from twilight until dawn in unlit alleys, chaos all around.

"Not true," Bathsheba's father wrote from Boston. Most of these reports were rubbish, he assured her, outright fabrication. "Unfortunately," he added, "denials and attempts to disprove the allegations as usual only serve to make bad matters worse."

Mrs Stratten brought home *The Boston Chronicle.* "There it is, ma'am," she told her mistress. "Read it for yourself." Governor Bernard was about to be appointed Governor of Virginia, and Hutchinson would take his place. Tim Ruggles, in turn, would become Lieutenant Governor.

"Pure fiction," Bathsheba countered. "They'll print anything to sell a paper."

With Ruggles back in the news, Sam Adams took the opportunity to rail again against him and the 17 rescinders, and, predictably, as a result, only five, the Brigadier among them, were re-elected in the '69 elections. In the end, only he and one other had the courage to show up in the General Court. Not that they could do much; they were all but powerless.

Gage finally gave in to harassment from Bostonians and the press, and removed half the troops from Boston's streets. Things quieted, and got even quieter when, in July, news arrived by ship that all the duties of the Townshend Acts had been repealed, except the tax on tea. Tensions were still further eased when Governor Bernard, exhausted by the battering he was suffering from the Whigs, was granted his request to be recalled to London.

The last day of July, scheduled for his departure, was darkened by no ordinary storm. Lightning forked into the harbor, splitting the masts of several ships. When the thunder and the waves subsided, Bernard made it out as far as Castle William, where he spent the night. By dawn, the storm was gone, the water in the harbor still, too still, the wind dead, and the *Rippon*, waiting to take the retreating Governor back to England, was becalmed for the next three days. Bernard had no choice but to listen to the church bells clanging on the mainland as part of Boston's celebration over getting rid of him.

Chapter 12

Girl, girl, Tory girl,
Aren't you sorry
Your ma's a Tory
And your granddad is a traitor.

Elizabeth crouched, her head between her knees, her back to the barrage of snowballs. She had done nothing to bring on this assault, she was just trying to make a snowman in her own back yard. Her tormentors renewed their chant, *Girl, girl, Tory girl!* An icy chunk hit hard between her shoulders.

"Mama," she screamed, "Mama, Mama!" Within seconds, Bathsheba was at her side, gathering her up, cursing the retreating bullies. Heavy with her second child, she staggered a little as she carried her firstborn through the snow to the safety of the kitchen. She settled Elizabeth on a stool before the fire. "Don't pay those hoodlums any mind," she said. "Sit here now, cozily, while I warm some sugar water for you, love. And a slice of ginger bread?"

Joshua watched them, eyes narrowed. Thoughtfully, he stroked his mermaid pipe, and then, as if he'd had some kind of epiphany, he smiled and nodded. "Why hasn't it occurred to me before?" he whispered to himself.

A week later, Bathsheba, drained by hours in labor, lay beneath a feather comforter beside her newborn son. It was peaceful now, the storm much quieter, snow falling still, but gently. Occasionally a pale shaft of sunlight shot through a break in the clouds and brightened the chilly little room just off the kitchen. "What time is it?" she called to Mrs Stratten.

57

"Mid-afternoon, ma'am. And you brought to bed a full day ago." She stood in the doorway between the kitchen and the borning room. "I've fixed a cot here by the fire, ma'am, much warmer. Come, let me help you." Mrs Stratten settled her mistress where the warmth could reach her and placed the infant in the cradle by her side.

"Mr Spooner, has he come home yet?"

"No, ma'am."

"And Elizabeth?"

"She's still with her cousin. But I reckon your sister Martha will bring her back before it's dark, she'll be so wanting to see her new baby brother. And your sister, too, ma'am, will be wanting to see you." Mrs Stratten propped Bathsheba on a pile of pillows and ladled out a bowl of soup. "I'll stay, ma'am," she said, "until your husband comes, should you be needing anything."

By the time Joshua returned, Bathsheba was asleep, Elizabeth and the newborn infant dozing close by. He considered them a moment, then followed Mrs Stratten to the kitchen door. "Before you go," he said, "I want to make a new arrangement."

She stopped midway in reaching for her cape. "Sir? Has my service not given satisfaction?"

"No, no, it isn't that." He handed her her scarf. "Have you noticed how Elizabeth clings to Mrs Spooner? I daresay it will be the same with this new one."

"Oh yes, sir, Elizabeth is Mrs Spooner's life. The mistress, she is often lonely, sir. And now, with this little son, well, you see how it is." She glanced at the sleeping mother and her children. "It's beautiful."

"Yes, but it has to change. It's not healthy. Strong attachments with one's children lead to trouble in the future."

"Oh, I'd not say that, sir. It's quite natural."

Joshua's glare stifled her argument. "You have a daughter," he said. "You've brought her here sometimes. A pretty girl." He smiled his smile. "I want her to take over with the children."

"Oh, sir. I don't think the mistress would like that. And Rebecca's young, sir, fourteen only. Able, though, I must admit, beg pardon, sir."

"Old enough. Bring her around."

"What possessed you?" Bathsheba demanded. Over the course of the past months, she had become convinced that Joshua's motives, whatever they might be, did not include a genuine concern for her.

"You need help," he insisted.

Her eyes searched his for the real explanation. "Why?"

"It's done. The arrangements have been made." He looked past her and lit his pipe.

Further discussion would be useless and almost surely hurtful, so she turned away, pondering, trying to understand. One possible reason kept surfacing. Of course, maybe she was wrong; her relationship with Joshua was so ridden with suspicion, it was hard to tell. But, maybe, just maybe, he expected this wedge between her and the children to bring him the kind of satisfaction he seemed to crave. He knew she would suffer from loss of their affection. Yes, Joshua was quite capable of conceiving a plan like that.

Her jaw jutted out in defiance, and a resolve to protect herself began to harden.

The next morning, Rebecca came as Joshua had ordered. Bathsheba led the girl to the infant's cradle. "The baby, Little Josh," she said simply. "Don't worry about him. I'll keep him in my care."

"But, ma'am...," Rebecca stammered. "The master gave strict instructions that you should not be troubled."

"That's not quite reasonable, now, is it? I'll be nursing him for months. No one is going to change that. Understood?"

"But the master said..."

"Come now, we don't want trouble. I will tend to Little Josh, let's you and I agree. We will be prudent how we manage it, just between us, Rebecca." She touched the girl's lips to seal the secret. "Now help

Elizabeth with her boots and wraps, and take her for a scamper in the snow."

Bathsheba stood with the baby in her arms, watching from a window in the sitting room. Two children at play, Rebecca lying in the snow demonstrating how to make snow angels with huge wings, the little girl laughing, sweeping out a baby angel beside Rebecca's big one. They ran about, disappeared behind the house, then re-appeared, dragging the sled that once had been Bathsheba's, and heading toward the slope near Hinckley's house. She smiled, remembering the joy of snow, the excitement of sliding down the hill behind her father's stables, and, when she was older, the thrill of bob-sledding with Nathan.

Mrs Stratten brought the news, scarcely able to contain herself. "A massacre, ma'am, that's what they're calling it, smack in the middle of Boston, men and boys shot dead. No telling how many. No doubt, though, that it was the Bloodybacks that did it."

Bathsheba's eyes flashed. "Without any provocation, I suppose!"

"There's no knowing, ma'am. It's all confusion."

Two days later, Mrs Stratten came to work with a cartoon. "There's a pile of 'em at the general store, tuppence each. I thought you'd like to see." *The Bloody Massacre perpetrated in King Street Boston on Marth 5th, 1770 by a party of the 29th Reg't. Engrav'd Printed & Sold by Paul Revere Boston.* There it was, vivid and inaccurate, seven Redcoats lined up firing at a group of innocent civilians, some down and others falling.

What next? Would events in Boston rage beyond control again, breeding uncertainty and fear throughout the colony? "The world is skidding," Bathsheba told Bridie as she curried the animal. "And I risk going down with it." She had a great desire to go to Hardwick, find Nathan, and spill out all her troubles, open up at last, forget propriety, be comforted. But she stopped short; she must be mad even to think such things. Over a week ago, Mrs Stratten had informed her that banns had been posted for Nathan and Susanna White. She, Bathsheba, had no claim on him. She never did.

Chapter 13

Throughout the spring and summer of 1770, Sam Adams continued his struggle to gain control of Massachusetts, but with slight success, and in the fall the outcome of the massacre trials was a further set-back to his cause. Prosecutor Robert Treat Paine proved to be no match for Sam's young cousin, John, the only lawyer in the town of Boston who would agree to defend Captain Preston and the soldiers charged with firing on the citizens. Although far from being a pro-British advocate, John Adams argued brilliantly and fairly for his clients, and in the end secured the acquittal of the Captain, and, in a separate trial, the same for all but two of the accused men in his regiment. Even they received only a mild sentence: branding on the hand for manslaughter.

Once the trial was over, Boston, weary of contention, settled down, essentially ignoring the blizzard of diatribes published by Sam Adams in the *Gazette*. Acting Governor Hutchinson had reason to breathe a little easier, although he still had to contend with a General Court that, having refused to function under the guns of the Regulars in Boston, had been moved by Governor Bernard to Cambridge. There the legislators sat, still doing nothing, and, with this impasse, the Brigadier—chosen again by Hardwick, but this time by a narrow margin—decided it wasn't worth his while to attend. The Royal cause was all but lost, at least in Massachusetts.

By the late spring of 1772, Bathsheba knew that she again was pregnant. She did not want another child, this one conceived in a fit of Joshua's lust. Her condition made her ill, she hated it. Add to that her increasing isolation. Women crossed the road when they saw her coming. Her children were spending more and more time with

Rebecca, just as Joshua had planned. Her father no longer came to Brookfield; he excused himself by saying he was nothing but a detriment, what with people spreading malice everywhere he went; even the Hardwick citizens no longer chose him as their representative, sending no one to the General Court rather than send him. Sheba had long since broken off her visits; she never had liked Joshua, she never would, and he did not like her. Bathsheba longed for Uncle John, but she hesitated to invite him for fear Joshua might treat him badly.

Yet, despite her general malaise, Bathsheba still followed news reports and she took some heart from rumors that Sam Adams was losing the support of the Boston merchants. He could talk non-importation all he wanted, and for awhile they'd gone along with him, but now they were convinced that his policies were bringing them to ruin. Enough was enough.

Good.

But then, in late fall, events played into his hand again when the Crown decreed that henceforth it would pay provincial judges, thereby making them beholden. Sam Adams grabbed his chance. Using his new Committee of Correspondence, he took his message directly to the people, broadcasting reports about British infringements of American rights, some real, some imagined.

From her third child's first hour, it was clear to Bathsheba that he wasn't right. When she put him to breast, he refused, his tiny fingers moving frantically. She sat with him for hours, stroking his head, coaxing him to nurse, but then, almost immediately, he would vomit projectiles of curdy milk and mucus. Each day his appearance became more frightening, his small head shrinking until it was nothing but a skin-covered skull with sunken eyes.

The fault must somehow lie with her, for it was an evil thing not to want a baby, and she had not wanted this one. Maybe it was her resentment that had made her ill and in turn had harmed the babe. Maybe her milk was bad, turned rancid by his piercing shrieks.

The child was suffering so, he broke her heart. Nothing she did helped, not in the slightest way, so finally, defeated, she handed him to Mrs Stratten, hoping for a miracle. She watched her try to feed him cow's milk from a papboat, but nothing changed.

"He should be bled," Mrs Stratten said when all her efforts failed.

"No!" Bathsheba did not hold with bleeding; her mother had always been against it. "Absolutely not!"

"Ma'am, I only meant … I mean, I thought it is the only thing to do when matters get so serious like this."

"You're right," Joshua agreed, and prepared to set out for the doctor.

"No! Even a fool can see he needs every drop of blood he has."

"Good doctors always bleed their patients. You know nothing about medicine."

"Stop! Please Joshua. Stop!"

The infant was by now too weak to cry, and Mrs Stratten wrapped him in a coverlet, took him to the sitting room, and shut the door against the growing argument.

A little later, Baby John died in Mrs Stratten's arms.

"The burden of his passing is on you."

Bathsheba bent over the emaciated corpse, dry eyed, not hearing.

"You are to blame."

I am to blame, I'm culpable. My animus toward Joshua wronged the infant, and now he's dead from some malformation that curled inside his tiny body, something I must have caused. I am to blame!

Barely aware of who or where she was, Bathsheba joined Mrs Stratten to lay out the corpse. Jesse made a crude pine coffin, and Baby John was buried the next morning in a plot down by the brook. No one was present but the family, Mrs Stratten, Jesse, and Rebecca. If any prayers were said, they were drowned by the raw March rain, shredded by the wind.

As Jesse lowered the remains into the little grave, Joshua turned, bent low like an old man, and walked away, sobbing audibly.

Joshua, oh Joshua!

Day followed day. It was cold in the east parlor where Bathsheba sat alone for hours. Mrs Stratten intruded periodically, bringing food and tea, offering the *Gazette.* "You might care to read about your father's friend. He's in trouble again, ma'am."

It seemed that Hutchinson had made some confidential, ill-advised remarks about the province in a communication to a Mr Whately in London. After Whately's death, the letters made their way across the ocean and eventually reached Boston where they fell into the hands of Samuel Adams. Inevitably, he found in them a plot against America. Rumors spread, caught fire, and soon mere inferences became official fact. Now, the *Gazette* proclaimed, Adams was calling for petitions to the King to get rid of Hutchinson.

The report served to rouse Bathsheba, just a little at first, but slowly she began to see beyond her grief. By the time the crocuses began to bloom, she had resolved to start anew, and when Joshua informed her that he would be away for several weeks, she wrote to Uncle John, begging him to visit. "I don't mind being alone, and I often cherish private time, especially with Bridie, riding free," she said in closing. "But now I'm a bit lonely, sometimes melancholic, and in need of you."

Chapter 14

The designated day was perfect, warm at last. Bathsheba took a book to the back garden to wait for Uncle John. She loved the wild beauty that surrounded her, tulips and late daffodils, violets and hyacinths, blending their fragrances and hues against the backdrop of the hills, miles away and tender green. She thanked heaven that Joshua's business—or something—had taken him away, giving her time to be with Uncle John, to talk, to walk, to let him get acquainted with the children.

Rebecca came out and spread a white cloth on the low table near the bench that ringed the maple tree. "Join us when it's time for tea," Bathsheba said.

"Oh, ma'am, I couldn't."

She is pitifully shy, Bathsheba thought, yet so eager to be helpful, do what is expected. But so uncertain with adults, especially now. It was understandable, of course, considering her circumstance. "Surely you can take your tea with us," Bathsheba coaxed. "You've met my uncle more than once. You took to him, I think."

Rebecca nodded vaguely.

Uncle John was seldom late, and true to form, he arrived at precisely two o'clock. He greeted his niece with tears and kisses. "How beautiful you are," he said. "You always have been beautiful. Where are your little ones?"

"Just up from naps, no doubt. Rebecca will bring them presently."

He glowed with pleasure when they ran to him. He took from his pocket a small wooden ball on which he'd carved the image of a butterfly. "You'll soon be old enough for me to help you catch some real butterflies," he said as he handed it to Little Josh. He gave

Elizabeth a book he'd made, with sketches of the treasures in his secret room, Bathsheba's favorite place. "You see," he said, "I've written a story to go with every drawing."

"The same tales you used to spin for me?" Bathsheba asked.

"Elizabeth is growing up like you," he said.

They talked about the pleasantness of spring, about the looming possibility of war, about the Brigadier, carefully avoiding mention of the loss of Baby John. They strolled through the garden. "Are you doing any new experiments?" Bathsheba asked.

"Oh, yes. Have you heard about that Philadelphia man? I've read what he wrote about his kite. But I won't try that. Very dangerous, you know, he might have been struck dead."

"No extra cup?" Bathsheba asked when Rebecca brought the tea things. "Well, sit down, anyway. Uncle John enjoys a bit of chatting."

"She's right," John said. "I am a talker."

Rebecca offered a plate of tea cakes to the children.

"You like young ones, I can see," John said.

"Yes, sir, I do."

"And I can see you soon will have a baby of your own. I'm glad for you." John beamed at her.

Rebecca stiffened. Her lips parted as though she was about to speak, but nothing came, and John noticed that her hands were bare of rings. He glanced over to his niece; she shook her head.

"Oh dear," he stammered. "What a blundering fool I am." His eyes begged Rebecca for forgiveness.

"It's all right," Bathsheba said. It pained her to see him so upset. "I'm going to help her at the birth." She reached out and took Rebecca's hand, and was about to tell her that she shouldn't be afraid when she caught sight of Joshua. Oh God, he's back, already back, and this lovely visit is going to be spoiled. "I think Mr Spooner has come home," she said.

Rebecca stood up. "I'd best leave, miss," she said. She turned to flee, but not soon enough to escape Joshua's glance as he strode towards his wife.

He's about to do some terrible thing, Bathsheba thought.

He approached, arms akimbo, head cocked to the side. "I'm surprised," he said, addressing Uncle John in an accusing voice. "Surprised to find you here as Mrs Spooner's guest. She's not been feeling well of late and ought not to overdo."

Uncle John shook his head, confused. "I'm sorry, I didn't know, I mean…"

Bathsheba caught his hand. "Don't go," she said. "We've scarce begun our tea. I'm not unwell, not in the least." She challenged Joshua. "Perhaps it's you who's feeling poorly. At any rate, I invited Uncle John, I've been wanting him to visit now for months."

"No, no, I'd better leave," John said. "I really must. Yes, I must. I'll come back some other day, some summer day, some other time. I'm late. The shadows will grow long and the sun be getting low, and I've a long ride home. My little mongrel bitch has had a batch of pups, and she'll be needing me to get her dinner." He fumbled for his hat and blew a kiss in the direction of the children. "Goodbye, goodbye." He hugged Bathsheba. "Come to New Braintree for a visit." He bowed to Joshua and was gone.

Bathsheba faced her husband. "You're despicable!"

"I was only trying to protect you."

"For weeks I've dreamed of having time with Uncle John. He lifts my spirit. We love each other, Joshua, something you can't understand."

"No doubt. Well, I have no love for him, which he knows instinctively, although he's otherwise dull witted. I can't think what you see in him."

"Perhaps I'm better sighted than you are."

"I could see well enough that you were with that girl. It's not proper that you sit down with the help here in my garden, all dressed up and holding hands as if she were a friend. Drinking tea."

"We were not drinking tea!" Her voice was rising. "Rebecca refused it, and as for Uncle John and me, we didn't have a chance to take a sip! You delight in ruining any pleasure I might have. Don't you, Joshua? Don't you! That makes you happy, doesn't it?"

"She's beneath you." He came close. "Keep your distance from Rebecca Stratten. Remember that!"

Remember, yes. He's quite capable of finding ways of making one remember. He's capable of anything. Trembling with anger tinged with fear, she led the children past their father, in from the fragrant afternoon, through the kitchen to the borning room. She kicked the door shut and threw the bolt. Breathing hard, she gathered Elizabeth and Little Josh into her arms and pressed them close. The children began to cry. She straightened with a rush of strength. "This won't do," she said. "Dry your tears. Let's go to Bridie. You each can ride her for awhile. That will cheer you up, now, won't it?"

After the mare had carried the children from the barn out to the meadow, back and forth ten times each, Bathsheba gave them over to Rebecca. "I'll be back before nightfall," she said. If she rode at a fast clip, there would be time to get to Hardwick to regain composure by the stream where she and Nathan used to meet.

Chapter 15

The following Saturday, Mrs Stratten came to work distraught. "Rebecca can't come today, she's not good, her ankles big as stumps, and headaches all the time. Says her seeing's blurred as well, and she scarce can keep a cracker down."

Jesse, coming from the milk room, heard. "She'll be all right, won't she?"

Bathsheba had long suspected that he was smitten by the girl, although he was too shy to even speak to her. But whenever Rebecca was around, he stopped whatever he was doing just to gaze at her. He worshipped her and didn't seem to mind when everyone could see that she was carrying a child that he knew for sure was not his.

"Don't fret," Bathsheba told him. "It's not unusual for a girl to feel poorly as her time draws near." An easy thing to say.

Early one morning about a fortnight later, sister Martha arrived breathless at the kitchen door. "Rebecca's pains have started," she announced. "Before dawn her mother came to me and asked if I would fetch you. The girl is asking for you, and they both would feel relieved if you would come. They can't afford a midwife."

With Joshua's warnings still echoing in her head, Bathsheba gathered up the things that she would need, not forgetting to include a flask of Joshua's rum. Dear God, she thought, don't let him wake before I get away.

"I might be quite awhile," she said to Martha, speaking softly. "Thanks for taking over with the children. She found Jesse in the barn, just finishing the milking. "You'd better come with me," she told him. "You might be needed."

"Yes, ma'am!"

He desperately wants to help, Bathsheba thought.

Seconds later, standing in his nightshirt at the window of their chamber, Joshua watched his wife ride down the road on Bridie, Jesse running after.

Bathsheba found Rebecca fully clothed lying on her narrow bed. Her eyes were sunken, her straight blond hair tangled and damp with sweat. Seized by cramping pain, she grabbed the towels tied to the bedpost, and pulled until her muscles bulged.

Remembering her own ordeals, Bathsheba cradled the girl's face between her palms. "When it's over and you hold your baby in your arms, all this will be as nothing."

"No." Fear clouded Rebecca's eyes. "I'm going to die."

Jesse, standing just outside the doorway, blanched.

Bathsheba searched in her satchel, got out the flask of rum, and handed it to Mrs Stratten. "Fix a strong drink," she ordered. "I've brought some herbs as well." She removed Rebecca's bonnet and untied her laces.

An hour of periodic pain went by, and then another, but the baby made no progress. Noon came and went. Bathsheba prepared tea and toast and tried to tempt Rebecca. I mustn't show how worried I am, she thought. I mustn't frighten her. But by mid-afternoon she knew that she should wait no longer, and she called Jesse. "Take Bridie and fetch Mrs Harding." She turned to Mrs Stratten. "It's only a precaution." She hoped she sounded reassuring. "Don't worry, I will pay."

Fifty years of age, with eleven children of her own and long experience with birthing, the midwife soon inspired confidence. She sat down beside the bed and took Rebecca's slender hand. "I'll need to probe a bit," she said. "It's nothing to be frightened of." Then after she had finished, she took Bathsheba to one side. "The babe's in an unnatural position," she said. "But I think that I can bring things right." She clearly knew her business, and worked calmly and with

71

purpose while Mrs Stratten and Bathsheba stood by with soothing words and sips of rum for the suffering girl. They cooled Rebecca's forehead with wet rags.

"Tell me who the father is," Mrs Harding said after an especially strong contraction. "I'm duty bound, you know."

"Yes, I know. I've been expecting you to ask." Rebecca's voice was scarcely audible. "I know that you're just following the law. But I can't, I can't!"

Mrs Harding tried again. "Surely you don't want to be despised because your bastard is a burden to the town." Her attitude was gentle, but her voice was stern. "That's how its going to be, you understand, if the Select Men don't know where to lay responsibility."

"It would be easier for you, I think, if you would tell," Bathsheba urged. "You'd be doing what is right."

But Rebecca whispered, "No."

Throughout the afternoon, Mrs Harding checked her patient frequently, and after one of her examinations she took Bathsheba to the kitchen and shut the door. "I think perhaps the child no longer is alive," she said. "I'll do everything I can to get this over with." She called to Jesse: "I'd be obliged if you would fetch my other saddlebag."

She chose from it an extract of marigold and snakeroot and gave it to Bathsheba. "Have Rebecca drink this freely," she said. "It ought to take hold soon. Meanwhile, I'll catch a rest."

It was almost dark by now, and Mrs Stratten lit two candles and her Betty lamp. Shadows trembled on the walls. The intervals between the periods of Rebecca's agony grew shorter until finally, by calling on all her past experience, Mrs Harding wrested the baby from its mother's womb. She looked at Mrs Stratten, slowly shook her head, and handed the dead infant to Bathsheba.

There was trouble with the afterbirth, and when, in the dead of night, it was at last expelled, Rebecca's blood raged out. Dark stains spread across the bedding. Soon all the cloths that Mrs Stratten had laid by were soaked, and she grabbed anything that she could lay a hand to—a towel, a shirt, an apron, anything to staunch the flow. To Bathsheba, working at Mrs Harding's side, the floors, the walls, the ceiling seemed to blur together into one smeared bloody mass.

As a last resort, Mrs Harding chose a vial of purple powder that she'd ground from Amaranthus petals. "Mix this with water, and insist Rebecca drink it all." But the potion did not help. By now congealed clots were coming out, like pieces of raw liver. Bathsheba shook her head to clear it as she struggled for control.

Slowly the hemorrhaging abated, and the dying girl lay white and motionless. She's drained, unconscious now, Bathsheba thought. But when she left the room to find clean sheets, Rebecca raised her hand, ever so slightly, and beckoned Mrs Harding to come close. She managed only a few words.

Over her thirty years of midwifery, Mrs Harding had become almost inured to shock, but this time her features froze. "You're telling true?" she asked. She glanced at Mrs Stratten; her face was ashen. Rebecca closed her eyes. "I'm thirsty."

Mrs Harding ordered Jesse to fetch fresh water from the well. He hurried to do as he was told, but after he had passed the dipper to the midwife, something in him snapped. Blazing with fury, he raced from the house into the damp approaching dawn, shouting curses on the man, whoever he might be, who had violated his Rebecca and brought on such suffering.

The only sound was from the dripping candle wax. Bathsheba wrapped the little corpse in the coverlet Rebecca had quilted with such care to keep the infant warm, but now a shroud. Soon death will claim Rebecca too, Bathsheba thought. She watched Mrs Stratten stroke her daughter's cheek, her lips moving in silent prayer.

The deathly quiet was broken by the sound of horse's hooves, slowing now, and stopping at the kitchen dooryard. Bathsheba left Rebecca's side and stood facing Joshua astride his horse, seemingly much larger than he was. Cruel.

"So you went to her!" His words came out like gunshots aimed across the threshold. "I saw you leaving yesterday, and when I pressed her, Martha told me where you'd gone. I waited, thinking you'd remember that I warned you. All day I waited, on into the evening. I considered coming here to fetch you after I had said goodnight at Cooley's, but I was weary."

Drunk, Bathsheba thought. Dead drunk.

"Martha left, said she could stay no longer. I fell asleep. But by now I've had enough. Come back where you belong before your children waken and find no one at home."

She must appease him somehow. There mustn't be a scene, not here, not now. "I had no desire to cross you," she said. "I thought you'd understand how much Rebecca needed me." She went back into the house. "I must go," she murmured. "I'll come back." She approached Mrs Harding, who was standing at the kitchen door, staring at Joshua with obvious contempt. "I'll bring your fee as soon as possible," she whispered. "How much?"

"My usual is six shillings, ma'am, but this time was especially hard."

"I'll bring you twelve."

She embraced Mrs Stratten, brushed by her husband, and mounted Bridie.

A little later she stood facing Joshua in his sitting room. "The baby's dead." She stared past him at the red-grained fireplace bricks. Dried blood, she thought. "And Rebecca's dying." She sat down, every bone aching, even breathing was an effort.

Joshua stood over her. "I've been giving you a lot of thought," he said. He picked up his meerschaum pipe and slowly ran his fingers the full length of the carved mermaid.

His smile is full of evil, Bathsheba thought. She did not move or speak, just stared at him and waited. He finally went to the back door. "Jesse!" he called out, but Jesse did not answer. "Lazy lout!"

"Leave Jesse be! He was there with us, and he was much affected. He is suffering." But no one's suffering means anything to Joshua, she thought. No one's suffering but mine, in which he takes his pleasure.

He shouted louder, and this time Jesse came, looking grey and as if he'd lost his bearings. "Saddle my horse, and tether Bridie to him," Joshua ordered. He turned to Bathsheba. "Last night I met someone at Cooley's who was looking for a horse. I thought maybe that's the answer, maybe that would bring you round. So I made a deal with him."

Bathsheba drew in her breath. She grabbed Joshua's arm. "Please don't!" Her eyes beseeched him. "Anything but this!"

He smiled and pushed her off. "At last," he said. "Good."

She could not bear to watch as he rode off at a slow trot with Bridie close behind, balking intermittently.

Chapter 16

Tea! Bathsheba poured scalding water onto a spoonful of green leaves that Mrs Stratten had managed to bring home from the black market. Tea and taxes! Bathsheba took her cup and the *Gazette* to the settle by the fire.

"On Thursday just past," the newspaper announced, "three shiploads of tea were dumped in Boston Harbor."

A special town meeting, called to prevent the unloading of the tea ships, was attended by so large a crowd that expediency required it to be moved from Faneuil Hall to Old South Church. Mr Josiah Quincy spoke with eloquence, making it clear that war could not any longer be avoided. Mr Samuel Adams brought matters to a head with a signal for action. "This meeting," he announced, "can do nothing more to save the country." Within minutes, an orderly band of faithfuls, dressed as Mohawk Indians, boarded the Dartmouth, the Eleanor, and the Beaver, and took over without resistance. By the time they finished, the harbor was clogged with the contents of 342 chests of tea, worth £18,000 sterling. The group disbanded without violence, and gentle waves, glutted with tea leaves, lapped quietly in the moonlight.

So this is what the Tea Act has accomplished! Quite a different story from its intended bail-out of the East Indian Tea Company, whose warehouses were bulging with rotting tea because the American market had hit rock bottom. Not that the Americans had taken an aversion to the beverage; they loved their tea, but preferred to get it from enterprising smugglers who not only sold for a much better price, but also did not impose the lingering Townshend tax. The Tea Act was meant to put a stop to this by granting the East India Company a monopoly on the tea trade and allowing it to export directly to the colonies. With the English and American middlemen cut out, the Company could drastically reduce the price, and Parliament expected Americans to rejoice and abandon smugglers in favor of East Indian tea.

Fine. Except there was still a tax, three pence a pound, a prickly thorn. Moreover, if this monopoly thing was happening with tea, what would prevent its happening with all manner of other goods in which the Company traded?

American merchants, forced out of the loop, were roused to a pitch, full of dire predictions. Would they not, after all, be driven into bankruptcy? In a panic, they turned back to their one-time friend, and again Sam Adams saw an opportunity to promote his cause. By this time, he had in place Committees of Correspondence in almost every Massachusetts town, and through them he could get out his message: stop malevolent Britannia in her tracks. "Tea and taxes" was the battle cry. "No taxation without representation" was a powerful slogan, and when the three tea ships arrived in Boston harbor, Adams' men, backed by compatriots in the countryside, were prepared for action.

When news of Boston's Tea Party reached London, Parliament immediately lashed back with the Coercive Acts of 1774, which overturned the Massachusetts Charter of 1729, and revoked the liberties it guaranteed. Governor Hutchinson was ordered to London to account for Massachusetts' misbehavior, and British General Gage was brought in to replace him. Most importantly for Bathsheba and her father, the Governor's Council, formerly elected, was abolished and replaced by a Mandamus Council composed of Gage's appointees. The Brigadier had the terrible misfortune to be one of them. Although most of the other designated men refused, he accepted, and as the summer of 1774 was drawing to a close, he prepared to go to Boston and be sworn in.

Bathsheba was on the road to Hardwick soon after dawn, but the August heat was already bearing down. She would have to pay one way or another for riding off like this, on a horse she'd borrowed from Captain Weldon. She was pregnant again, and Joshua was sure to accuse her of risking the life of their unborn child. But nothing could stop her. She would ride with care, she would not harm the babe. She had to see her father to say goodbye. He was at the top of the rebels' list of Tory traitors, and she was well aware of the danger he was in; she knew about the threats against his property and life. Moreover, she was sure that as long as the rebels had the upper hand, he could never return to Hardwick except on pain of death.

The Ruggles household was in great confusion, and Bathsheba had only a few minutes alone with her father, stolen time, in the stables, while he prepared Midnight for the ride ahead. "Don't go to Boston," she pled. "Gage can get along without you. You have done enough for the Royal cause. Please."

"Don't worry about me. Remember that I'm doing what I must."

He's stubborn and intractable, she thought, a fighter to the end.

He glanced at her thickened waist and raised his eyebrows with a question.

She nodded.

"Well then, all's well family-wise?"

"Yes." No point in saying otherwise.

A little while later, the Brigadier, in full military regalia, rode slowly down his long driveway through the humid heat. Bathsheba's brother John was with him, as well as the family carpenter and several loyal servants who had begged not to be left behind. Bathsheba followed on foot, the only other member of the family. She wondered at the duplicity of men as she nodded to neighbors who in better days had been her father's friends, but were now lined up along the road, standing in silent condemnation.

Then, a little way ahead, she caught sight of Nathan, and saw him smile at her father. Eight years, she thought, her eyes stinging from emotion. Eight years since she and Nathan said goodbye. But she'd kept track of him, sometimes through her mother, sometimes Mrs Stratten. And, yes, as her lot worsened, she had yearned for him. He's as dependable as ever, she thought, as he gave a wave of encouragement to her father. As she passed by him, her eyes locked with his, and only the solemnity of the occasion kept her from leaving the procession to embrace him.

The drummer of the town militia brought everybody to attention. The men, many of them carrying guns, took their positions in a show of force—a warning to the Brigadier that, once he left, his life would be in jeopardy if he returned. His brother Benjamin stepped forward from the crowd and held up his hand. "Timothy!" he said, as the Brigadier reined in his horse. "Stop, I beg you, and reconsider."

Papa! Bathsheba wanted to cry out, I need you here far more than you are needed by the Governor!

"Don't leave to serve on the damned Council," Benjamin continued. "A time of desperate conflict is approaching. Stay with us, it's useless to oppose the changes that must come."

The Brigadier stood massive, silent, his lips set in a narrow line. The only sound was a long whiney from his horse. In another try at reaching him, Benjamin took a personal approach. "Listen to me," he said in a low voice. "In the name of all that we have done together, all the good times and the bad, for our father's memory, for Sheba's sake, for all your children, I beg you not to go. We've loved each other many years. We're neither of us young. If you go, it will be the end between the two of us, and between you and the family that you leave behind. It's too late in life to rupture all your ties."

"Listen to him," Bathsheba called out. "Listen!"

But she knew he would not heed her. His integrity, his loyalty, and his instincts as a fighter all demanded that he go to Boston and take his oath without regard to private consequences. No threats of personal loss would weaken his commitment. "Goodbye, Benjamin," he said.

"If you cross that bridge this morning, you'll not cross it again alive!" Benjamin inclined his head in the direction of the militia.

"You are wrong! When I'm ready, I'll come back, leading five hundred soldiers, if need be."

The two brothers faced each other, two statues carved from granite. After a long minute, the Brigadier made a stiff, uncompromising bow, and Benjamin, defeated, signaled the militia to break ranks and let the entourage pass through.

It's done, it's over, Bathsheba thought. She felt wooden, as when Baby John had died. She turned, then stumbled, and would have fallen had not a strong hand reached out to steady her. "The Brigadier will be all right," a voice behind her said. "But you? How are you?"

Tears threatened as she placed her hand in Nathan's. But she could not tell him how she was, she could not speak about her need for him, she couldn't talk about her father and how alone she felt without him. Not here, not now, not ever. Yet she ought to make some comment, anything to let him know that she appreciated his concern. "Mama tells me that your two little sons are beautiful," she said. "How is Susanna?"

"My wife and family are fine." Then, "Sometime this fall I might need to come to Brookfield. Your husband is the only man around who can still get Bohea tea. It's in great demand, you know, despite the contraband." His smile was like a balm to her. "Perhaps I'll see you when I come to pick it up," he added.

"Yes." It would be heaven to talk with Nathan for awhile, erase the years between, if only for an hour.

Chapter 17

Nathan did not come, but one afternoon in late September, six weeks after the Brigadier left Hardwick, Mrs Stratten brought Bathsheba a thick letter that Jesse had picked up at the general store. "He happened to be there when the post rider came from Hardwick," she said. She bent close and lowered her voice. "I think he must have pinched it, ma'am, for he wouldn't be having the money on him to pay the rider, would he now? But he wanted to do you a favor. He's ever so fond of you."

Bathsheba noticed the address—or addresses, really. Her mother's name and "Hardwick," written in her father's familiar hand, had been lined through and replaced by Sheba's scrawl: "Please forward to Bathsheba Ruggles Spooner, Brookfield." She slipped the letter in her pocket and went to the east parlor. Without a fire, the room was chilly, but it was a place where she could be alone to savor her father's words.

She broke the seal. In the narrow margins, Sheba had managed to squeeze in a note. "I thought you'd like to see this. I think your father must be lonely. You'll notice at the end that he's distressed because you failed to answer the notes he sent you. I hope that doesn't mean that you're unwell."

Bathsheba looked up from her reading. She had received no letters, not from anyone, not in months. Could it be that Joshua...? No, even he would not stoop that low. Still, he was the one who always went to get the mail.

She dismissed the thought and began her father's letter.

Boston, 20 Septr., 1774

Dear Sheba,

By this time you must already know—everybody else in Massachusetts does—that our son John and I and the rest of our group made it to Boston without much incident. Barring, of course, the skirmish in Worcester, those damned Sons of Liberty trying to stop us from passing through. Mind you, I'm less frightened by the mobs than discouraged by the fact that the timing of their activities suggests some kind of central planning.

But enough of that! I know you must be anxious for a word about what's happened to Richard since he left Hardwick a week or so ago. I can put your mind at ease. He arrived in Boston safely, and I'm certain he will stay to help our cause in any way he can.

This wretched, overcrowded town is getting on my nerves. I never used to mind it, I suppose because I knew I could always get away. But that's no longer true, so I notice things that never bothered me before. The noise is worse than cannons in full fire, yelping dogs, squealing pigs, and carts and chaises rattling on the cobblestones like hell's hammers from dawn till dark. Vendors hawk all day, outshouting the town crier. Thieves are thick, and one always needs to be on guard, even at high noon. In a way, though, I have to hand it to them for their boldness. If they're caught, the gallows on the Neck stand ready, with an eager audience.

A few days after I was sworn in as a Mandamus Councilor, I took a notion to get out of here and go to Dartmouth to visit for a day or two with Colonel Tobey at his place on Buzzards Bay. I'd been advised against the trip, but I was damned if I'd let myself be holed up against my will. Looking back, I guess I have to say I didn't use good judgment, and I'm sure you would have been the first to say the same. I got to Tobey's in late evening to find that news of my arrival had preceded me. A mob, carrying torches and shouting their god-damns and various obscene threats, were there to greet me. I exploded, but when I realized that I was putting Tobey in a bad position, I told the crowd that I would leave, but not till morning. That delay proved to be a terrible mistake. At dawn I found Midnight in great distress. He had been painted red, his mane and tail cut off, and he died a few days later. You can imagine my fury and frustration, knowing I had no redress. The law is now entirely in the hands of the Committees, and they would never prosecute a case against a Son of Liberty for something as trivial as abusing a fine animal!

I think the Continental Congress down in Philadelphia will cause trouble. With Sam Adams there, anything might happen. At first, when we heard that he was going, some of us took heart, thinking that without his presence here, Massachusetts might shake off his grip. I've heard that he was worried about that too, but in the end, he could not miss an opportunity to seize power in a bigger sphere. Besides, he managed to get things well set up before he left. His new Committee on Safety is in place, and it's already making sure that every Massachusetts town has its militia in top shape. And I suppose you've heard about the so-called Minutemen. They are certain to cause trouble.

Even as I write, I'll wager that Adams is preaching American independence to anyone who'll listen. Despite him, though, I'm optimistic that people will regain their senses. Still, these are extraordinary times, and there are many who, for want of rational leadership, fall into the hands of madmen. We can only hope that Hutchinson will be returned to us from England, but I'm afraid that might not be. It's sad, not only for Massachusetts, but for him as well. He has written to me saying that he's homesick for the Province he was born in and he desperately hopes he can return, if only to be buried on his estate in Milton.

I forgot to mention that I'm trying to form an Association of Loyalists to take a stand against these so-called Congresses, Committees, and other unconstitutional assemblies. Incidentally, I've heard that brother Benjamin is heading Hardwick's newly constituted Committee of Correspondence. That's absolutely and forever the end between us.

Before I close, I want to mention that Bathshua didn't seem quite right to me that day when I left Hardwick. I've written to her twice, but I've had no reply. I'm worried about her, so please send me any news you have of her. Or better still, ask her to write directly. I can't deny, she is my favorite.

*Correspondence should be sent in care of
Governor Gage, the Province House, Boston.*

*As ever, Your husband,
Timo. Ruggles.*

Bathsheba read the ending of the letter several times. How wonderful to be a favorite! Her father had never told her that, but of course he wouldn't, it was not his style. But there had been signs, like the care he took in choosing Bridie, sparing no trouble or expense.

As for the missing letters, whatever might have happened to them, she owed it to her father to try to put his mind at rest. She went to the small desk in the sitting room. "Dear Papa," she began. Now what should she say? She couldn't bring herself to write that everything was fine, and she surely couldn't tell the truth. She could not write down in black and white that her husband was destroying her. For one thing, it would seem outrageous, not to be believed. So what should she say? Simply that she was all right and then tell an anecdote or two about the children.

She put her quill aside and gazed out at them playing beneath the maple tree. She tapped on the windowpane, but neither of them looked around. She called their names, "Elizabeth ... Little Josh." Whether or not they heard, they did not respond. They were as if on a stage, part of a pantomime that had no relevance to her. She longed to go to them, but she feared they would withdraw. They had grown estranged since Rebecca's death, turning to Mrs Stratten now for everything—Joshua's doing.

Chapter 18

The dazzling colors of the far-off hills were like a tonic to Bathsheba. The garden, too, was vivid, with banks of purple asters shining in the autumn sun, the day perfect for a walk, a long walk, hours and hours away from Joshua's house. She chose the road to Hardwick, not that she could go that far, but the way was pleasant and led to a place she loved.

Just beyond the church and graveyard, she came upon a company of militia drilling in a field and she paused to watch. Their weapons were of all descriptions, each man carrying whatever kind of gun he happened to possess, some without anything at all. The group was rag-tag, almost ridiculous, but their expressions were determined and defiant. Her father had led such men in the French and Indian war, and he used to say that every man in a New England training band understood exactly how and when to use his firearm. Although few of them liked war, they all would fight till death if they thought their way of life was threatened. Anything might happen if every militia in the colony was roused, not to mention what the Minutemen might do.

Bathsheba walked on, grateful that she had the road all to herself. She enjoyed the feeling of privacy in open space, and was annoyed when she saw a traveler in the distance riding toward her. But as he came nearer, she recognized him, and her irritation vanished. She ran to meet him.

He reined in his horse.

"This is a miracle!" she said, breathless with emotion.

"Actually, I'm on my way to your place." Nathan dismounted. "You've probably forgotten that when last we spoke—that day your father left last August—I mentioned that I might need to come to pick up some Bohea tea from Joshua."

"I did not forget. But as the weeks went by, I thought perhaps you'd changed your mind. I all but gave up the hope of seeing you again." He was even handsomer than she remembered.

"Fact is I did consider canceling the order." He sounded almost despondent. "I don't know how much longer I can keep my store. I've been too open with my views, and my customers are leaving one by one."

Her expression conveyed her sympathy.

"Well, nobody has threatened yet to ride me on a rail," he went on. "But I wouldn't be surprised. It's the damned Committees that keep riling people up. Do this. Don't do that. Don't trade with Loyalists." He glanced at her belly. "When is the baby due?"

"The beginning of the year." She felt somehow embarrassed, apologetic.

"Susanna is expecting too—our third."

Each of us with children, she thought, but not ours together.

"It's too bad you aren't going in my direction," he was saying. "We could walk a little way together."

"I wasn't really headed anywhere. I'll join you for a stretch."

They walked in silence for awhile. Then, "How's Joshua?"

She shrugged, and he nodded. "Refresh my memory," he said. "How old are your children now?"

"Elizabeth a little over seven and Little Josh is going on five. Did you know I lost a baby boy a year or so ago?" She reached out for Nathan's hand.

"I heard," he said. "Occasionally I visit your mother and get news of you. I should have written my condolences." He stopped and turned to her. "Can you accept them now?" Gently he placed his broad hands on her shoulders and kissed her forehead.

She brushed aside a tear. "It's your kindness," she apologized.

He asked about her father and she ran through the news in his recent letter. "I miss him," she concluded. "Terribly. Oh, Nathan, where is this all going? Where will it end?"

"In war."

She nodded.

Nathan seemed so close that for a moment Bathsheba considered mentioning the personal troubles that obsessed her, but, no, it would be better not to mar the deep communion that lay beneath their quiet conversation.

When they came to the ironworks just before the fork in the road that branched off toward Joshua's house, Bathsheba held out her hand. "Goodbye," she said. "You go ahead. I'm not ready to go home yet." She never would be ready, really.

A month passed before Nathan came again. "Dear God!" she exclaimed when she answered his familiar knock. His arm was in a sling, his cheek was bruised, and a nasty, jagged scab ran across his forehead. "I was mobbed," he told her. "Nearly killed." He explained that he had been attacked because he had refused to hand over to the rebels some tax monies he'd collected for the town. "They raised hell about it at town meeting, and I reacted, raging mad. Then when I started to walk out, they fell on me." He sneered his contempt. "I can take on one or two of those damned Sons of Liberty and do well," he went on. "But all the men in town—that's quite another matter. Do you remember Robinson, that six-foot, burly giant who lives on Hadley's farm? Well, he stepped in and saved my life. He told the mob he might not agree with how I handled things, but, by God, he did not agree with lynching either."

Nathan, dear Nathan. She ran her fingers from his injured forehead down his cheek. "Mrs Stratten brought home a tale that reached the Brookfield gossips. They said you were defiant about something—no one seemed to know quite what—and one day when the Hardwick Minutemen were drilling, you rode round and round the drill field, cursing them to hell."

"I did. Not very prudent for a man with a family to support."

"We all do and think things that aren't prudent." His narrow escape made her realize just how powerful her feelings were for him, and she was tempted to express them. "Leave your order," she said instead, avoiding Nathan's eyes. "You'll be picking up the tea yourself?"

Nathan came to Brookfield several times again, but by December most of Hardwick shunned his store, and he had little cause to deal with Joshua any more. But he dropped by one day on his way to Worcester to see Bathsheba and her newborn daughter. He asked her for advice, and he listened when she said she thought he should give in and close his store, it was hopeless trying to defy the rebels. His regard for her opinion cheered her, as it always had. Moreover, she was certain that he knew her life with Joshua was troubled. He could sense that something was the matter because he knew her heart.

Chapter 19

Bathsheba would always remember what kind of day it was, and exactly what she was doing when she heard the news on the afternoon of the 19th day of April, 1775. It was a Wednesday, and after two days of rain, the skies had cleared, and the temperature was almost balmy. She was sitting at the kitchen window, nursing Baby Bath and admiring the stand of daffodils in the dooryard when Mrs Stratten burst in. "The fighting's started! An express rider just came through from a town somewhere northwest of Boston. The militia all over Massachusetts have been put on the alert! Minutemen are already there."

The news hit hard. Although, like everybody else, Bathsheba had been half expecting this for months, now that it had happened, the reality did not seem real. She felt an urgent need to be alone and she handed Baby Bath to Mrs Stratten, and ran out into the sunshine, down the path past the barn, into the woods. She sat down by the brook and stared at the water rushing in full flood from the spring rains. Inevitable, she thought.

During the following week, bulletins kept pouring in, recounting tales about the battles at Lexington and Concord and the savagery of the retreat. On the rebel side, the militia, aided by householders along the way, harassed the battered British troops, killing or wounding hundreds as they stumbled back to their headquarters in Charlestown. The British, in turn, enraged by the Americans' barbaric sniping, defied their leaders' orders, and plundered houses, killed civilians.

Mrs Stratten brought back every scrap of news she heard. "'Tis past belief," she told Bathsheba. "The Redcoats ransacked a tavern in a town, Anatomy, I think it's called—or maybe I didn't get it right. It's on the road from Concord back to Boston. They butchered the owners, man and wife, and the two patrons who happened to be there. They cracked their skulls wide open, and spilled their brains out on the floor."

Reports soon followed that Boston was under siege, cut off from the mainland by rebels camped at both the Roxbury and Charlestown Necks. The Redcoats and government officials, all powerless now, were trapped, along with many Loyalists who had fled the countryside and taken refuge in the town before the fighting started. Papa's caught, Bathsheba thought. What will become of him and brothers John and Richard? There were rumors that the rebels planned to burn the town. Newspapers were hinting that they might infiltrate in the depth of night and pull off a proper massacre.

"We're all in danger now," Nathan said when he came to tell her that the Hardwick Committee had put her brother Timothy under house arrest and ordered him to pay for his own guard.

"And Mama?"

"She's holding out, angry and indomitable."

Months passed. The news from Boston worsened. By summer, food was getting scarce. Little could be smuggled past the rebel guards stationed on the mainland and all along the shore. By fall, the King's stores were practically depleted, and the Redcoat officers were eating rotting meat or sea gull stew. Civilians dined on cats and dogs. As winter settled in, building after building was torn down for firewood, until, in some areas, only chimneys still remained, stark against the winter sky.

"Thousands are sick or dying," Mrs Stratten reported. "Smallpox, they say. And there's them that got wounded at the battle at Bunker's Hill, taken off with the gangrene. Funeral carts are everywhere, ma'am, that's what they say. Both day and night. But General Howe forbids a decent tolling of the bells. Can you imagine? The mournful sound depresses him. It spoils the pleasure of his nights with the wife of the officer who runs his Commissariat, they say. Shameful, ma'am, I call it."

91

Bathsheba prayed to any god who'd listen. Keep Papa safe and free from pestilence, John and Richard, too, Would she get word, would her mother hear, if any of them were ill? Things were so mixed up, one couldn't count on anything.

In fact, the Brigadier and his two sons were faring as well as anyone in the beleaguered town. He still talked with people in high places—or what used to be high places—and he still spoke his mind. Months ago he had made it clear that he considered General Gage incompetent, and now he regarded his replacement as no better. With his usual directness, he gave General Howe some unsolicited advice. Dorchester Heights should be fortified before it was too late. "Its location overlooking both the town and harbor makes it critical," he warned. "The rebels are sure to move their forces there as soon as they are able, unless you do it first." But the idea of making an advance in freezing weather did not appeal to Howe.

With the rebels holding Boston captive, the Committees took charge in every other town in Massachusetts, excluding Tories from all social and commercial intercourse, frequently confining them, and confiscating any arms they might possess. Some were tarred and feathered, some ridden on the rail. Like many others under threats of death, Bathsheba's brother-in-law, Gardiner Chandler, and sister Elizabeth fled to England. The Hardwick Committee seized all the Brigadier's livestock, putting up for auction 20 horses, 30 head of cattle, also sheep and swine, the proceeds to be added to the rebels' war chests.

In early March of '76, General Washington did exactly what the Brigadier had predicted. Under cover of darkness, while rebel bombardments on the mainland diverted Howe's attention, the Americans built a fort of close-packed bales of hay on Dorchester Heights. A few days later, Howe woke up to face a battery of guns captured by American General Knox at Ticonderoga and hauled miles and miles to Boston over snow and ice. The sight of British ordnance aimed at British men-of-war in Boston Harbor was too much for Howe, and he turned tail.

Word that he was pulling out threw the town into a frenzy. There was no escape except by sea, and every boat owned by a Loyalist was commandeered. Barks, brigs, schooners, and sloops were jammed into the harbor alongside the British navy ships. The streets were clogged with carts and drays taking the possessions of the fleeing captives to the wharves.

On March 17th, thousands squeezed into the ships to which they were assigned, in some cases over thirty people wedged in cabins built for eight. The Brigadier and his sons were lucky, finding themselves with General Howe and a coterie of Redcoat officers on a relatively uncrowded war ship.

Captains shouted to each other and cursed as they struggled to disengage their vessels from their neighbors and move out to sea. Then, just eight miles off shore, Howe, in the lead, dropped anchor. There the flotilla stayed ten days, while the cargo, packed in frantic haste, was rearranged for safer sailing. From the deck, the Brigadier could just make out the Great Blue Hill in Milton, still topped with snow. It was there that his friend Hutchinson had built his country home where the Brigadier had often been a guest. Now it was a barracks for the rebels, and General Washington was traveling around in Hutchinson's fine carriage.

Finally, on the twenty-seventh day of March, Howe's fleet was ready. Gulls swooped among the vessels as gigs spread the news. "We're off to Halifax. Within the hour. All ships must stay together. Keep watch for enemy privateers, the waters are infested. All ships must stay together!" Sails were hoisted, anchors weighed.

If the Brigadier had been a man of sentiment, he would have wept as he watched the mainland disappear.

Chapter 20

A copy of the Declaration of Independence reached Brookfield on the fifteenth of July, and the Chairman of the town's Committee of Correspondence read it to the crowd gathered on the Common. Bathsheba was not among them; she would have been a fool to expose herself to the abuse that would certainly have been flung her way—insinuations, accusations, gestures. Loyalty to the King was now tantamount to treason.

Bathsheba's refusal to attend was not, however, due in any way to lack of interest. When the text of the Declaration was published in the *Massachusetts Spy,* she studied it with care. Many of its grievances seemed to her distorted or unfair, but the opening paragraphs struck home: "... certain inalienable rights... life, liberty, and the pursuit of happiness." Freedom and happiness. She'd almost forgotten what they were.

She laid the *Spy* aside and tried to concentrate on her design for a shift she was making for Elizabeth, but concern about her father and her brothers distracted her. They would be pilloried now more than ever. And what of us, the Loyalist women? Sacrifice and suffering lay ahead for everyone.

For everyone but Joshua. War won't make a bit of difference in his life, except, perhaps, to affect his income, one way or another. Nothing affects Joshua, his inner core. Some essential human traits were missing in his make-up, and she ought to be sorry for him. But compassion was impossible where Joshua was concerned.

Two sharp taps on the door, Nathan's way of knocking. Bathsheba felt a rush of pleasure in anticipation of a visit, but the moment she saw him, she knew from his expression that his news was bad.

"I've come to say goodbye," he told her. "The Sons of Liberty finally got their way. I've found it impossible to make ends meet without the store, with just the farm. I'm going to Maine."

She must not have heard correctly. All she could think of was how much it meant to her to have him drop by now and then, and Maine was far, too far for that.

"I'm sorry," he said. "I've little choice. I've let myself out at a good price to help manage an estate up in North Yarmouth, somewhat north of Portland."

If he had told her he was dying, she would not have been more stunned. She sat down heavily, and he sat down beside her and placed his hand on hers. "I'm sorry, Shua."

"Your family too?"

"No. At least not yet. Susanna will stay on with the children and run the farm. The Committee does not consider her as troublesome as me."

He must be desperate to even think of working for somebody else. "Who hired you?"

"Judge Jeremiah Powell. He needs extra help because he is away a lot in Boston. He's been appointed to the Revolutionary Council."

"You mean to say that you'll be working for a rebel? Have you gone mad?"

"He pays well and he hired me knowing full well I am a Loyalist. Proof, I guess, that not all rebels are fanatics."

"Maybe." Yes, it was possible. She recalled her father saying that some people in the part of Massachusetts known as Maine did not see things as black and white as did Bostonian Sons of Liberty. "How long will you be gone?"

"Until the work runs out, sometime in the fall, after the crops are harvested."

Months on end, endless months. Bathsheba turned away to hide her tears. "My father first, my brothers, and now you," she said.

Over the summer, news from the southern battlefields gave Loyalists reason for some hope. In late August, General Howe left Nova Scotia

95

for new battlegrounds and defeated General Washington at Brooklyn Heights, expelling him from New York City, booting him further south in pell-mell retreat. Loyalist militia were also winning local struggles in the area, and it seemed possible that they'd soon control the northern section of New Jersey. Reports reached Brookfield that up to five thousand Americans, led by the Brigadier, had come forward on Long Island to swear loyalty to the Crown. "Thank God," Bathsheba said to Mrs Stratten. "He'll turn things around, I'm sure,"

"Let's hope so, ma'am. If anybody can, he can. I remember tales of his leadership and bravery in the French and Indian War." For that the King had raised him to the rank of Brigadier General and given him grants of lands in Massachusetts and Vermont.

Fall came. The war was at a standstill. Tories and rebels alike were tense and uncertain as to what would happen next. Neighbors and family members who had been close a year ago, were breaking off relationships, not speaking, some shifting back and forth, never sure that they had chosen the right side. Joshua, typically, avoided making any choice, not coming down one way or the other, his lack of conviction filling Bathsheba with disgust.

There was, however, no question about the commitment of Hardwick's Committee. With revolutionary zeal, without proof, it charged Nathan with leaving town to serve the British as a spy, then seized his farm and leased it out while his family was still there. Later, when he returned from Maine in late November, they immediately arrested him, and by the first week in December, he was in the Worcester Gaol.

As soon as Bathsheba heard of this, she went to Captain Weldon. "I need a horse," she said. "Just for the day. I'll pay." She would find the money somehow, somehow steal it from Joshua.

"Don't worry, miss," the Captain said. "I'll lend you a mare, no payment needed."

The gaol loomed before her like a huge, grey cube, studded with oak joists filled in with stone and mortar, desolate and stark against a snow-filled sky. She secured the Captain's horse at the hitching post, banged the knocker on the iron door, and waited. Eventually the gaoler's wife peered through the peep hole and demanded who she was and why she'd come.

"Why would you be wanting to see that blackguard?" the woman asked.

"I've known him since I was a child."

"Wait a minute." The woman looked suspicious. "Aren't you...?"

She's recognized my name.

"I don't know. I'm not sure Mr Danforth should have visitors."

She really means she doesn't want to be accused of granting favors to a Loyalist.

"I need to ask my husband." The click of her heels on the granite floor receded.

Bathsheba paced the narrow path. Minutes dragged. Perhaps the gaoler's wife had no intention of returning.

At last the heavy bolt slid back. Thank God.

"This way," the woman beckoned. "We keep traitors down below. Your friend—if you want to call him that—has had the place all to himself since yesterday. Most scoundrels like him have seen the light and got on the right side of things."

Bathsheba followed, past the central fireplace and down the narrow passageway between the row of cells. A bearded man leered from behind a grill of iron bars, and whistled. The gaoler's wife sniffed. "He's in for fornication." They passed three others. "He's in for debt, him for theft, and him for forgery."

Although the gaol was only a quarter of a century old, the stone steps that spiraled to the dungeon were already worn, smooth and sloping. Bathsheba recoiled when she tried to steady herself by reaching out to the granite wall, slippery and slimy. She waited at the bottom while the woman searched among her keys.

"Ten minutes," the woman said.

Bathsheba shivered as she stepped into the dungeon. The acrid stench that rose from the dirt floor reminded her of stale wine and dead mice. For an instant she could not make out where Nathan was, but then, by the dim, flickering light from the central fire, she saw him coming toward her, shaking his head, incredulous.

He placed his hands on her shoulders, and this old familiar gesture was enough in itself to make the miserable trip worthwhile. "I've brought a little cake," she said, handing it to him. How inadequate, she thought.

"Having you visit here like this is the last thing in the world I would have dared to wish. Does your husband know you're here?"

She tossed her head. "It doesn't matter, I had to see you. How long are they going to make you stay here in this hole?"

"A few weeks, maybe more."

"Damn their stupidity!"

"Don't be too harsh. Take Curtis, for example. He was ordered to put me here, it wasn't his idea. He isn't a bad sort for a gaoler." Nathan picked up a sheet of paper from the straw mat on the floor. "See this," he said. "He gave it to me with a quill and ink so I can write a letter to Judge Powell."

Bathsheba's eyes widened with a question.

"The Judge appreciated what I did for him in Maine, and we parted on good terms. He's a fair man, and he knows the charge that I was spying for the British is rebel rubbish. He can testify for sure as to where I was and why, and he's in a good position to get me out on bond." Hands on his hips, Nathan looked confident. "I'm planning to bring suit against the Town of Hardwick, its Committee, and its Select Men, and they'll pay, by God!"

He's wonderful, she thought.

"And you?" he asked. "Here I am stuck in gaol, worrying about my family, and, yes, if the truth be known, worrying about you. How are things with you?"

She knew she shouldn't answer, but the words spilled out. "Nothing's any better, Nathan. Nothing ever will be. Sometimes I think I can't—or won't..." She gave him a desperate look. "I don't know what I'll do. Sometimes I scare myself, just thinking."

For awhile they said nothing, letting the tension from her outburst drain away. Then, "Hold fast, Shua. Remember the time—you were

98

about thirteen, I think—we'd been picnicking, you and I, your brothers, and a sister, too, Elizabeth, as I recall. Afterwards you insisted, laughing, impossibly defiant, you insisted on crossing the River Ware by crawling on a log that arched across the rapids. I could see that it was rotten, and I was frantic. I shouted not to be so headstrong or you'd drown. Do you remember what you answered?"

Bathsheba shook her head.

"You said more likely you'd be hanged. And that was not the only time I noticed what I think of as your strong life-wind, blowing away all reason and landing you in danger." He paused. "Promise to hold as steady as you can. And remember that I always will have faith in you."

Oh, Nathan, she thought, you raise my heart. I came here to try to help you somehow, but you don't need my help. It's the other way around.

She was bursting with gratitude, but before she could express it, the dungeon door creaked open.

"It's time." Mrs Curtis' keys clanked on their iron ring.

Bathsheba's eyes met Nathan's as he took her hand and squeezed it. "Thank you," she said. "More than I can say."

"It's time," the gaoler's wife repeated, with a jerk of her head in the direction of the door.

A fortnight later, on Christmas night, Washington led his troops across the Delaware into New Jersey, in weather so vile that no general in his right mind would even consider such a move. With the British troops off guard, relaxing over holiday libations, Washington took Trenton. Then, a few days later, he was victorious at Princeton, where he drank a New Year toast to 1777.

Chapter 21

Three months later
March, 1777

Bathsheba's woolen cape gave inadequate protection from the slicing wind, and the pale sunshine of the waning afternoon was cold. She cursed to herself as she struggled to keep the wheelbarrow, laden with a heavy bag of flour, from tipping over in the frozen ruts. Damn Joshua, he should be doing this. But he had refused and had made clear to Jesse that going for the flour was not part of his job. "Mrs Spooner will take care of it," he'd said. He knew how much she hated dealing with the miller, arrogant and condescending, the only tradesman allowed by the Committee to do business with a Tory. Joshua knew exactly how unpleasant these transactions were for her, which, she was sure, was why he forced them on her. She hated him for that.

Yes, hatred was consuming her. She was alone too much, or worse, alone with Joshua. Of course, there were the children, but Elizabeth and Josh were sufficient to each other. And Baby Bath, well, what can one expect from a child of two? There was no one to turn to. Nathan was back in Maine, having been released from gaol through the intervention of Judge Powell, who then rehired him. Even Mrs Stratten was away in Worcester with her niece, helping out with a new baby for God knows how long.

Bathsheba was negotiating a sharp turn when she heard shouts from Elizabeth and Josh as they burst around the corner of the house. "Mama! Daddy brought a sick man!" They trudged along beside the wheelbarrow, their faces alive at the prospect of some excitement in their lives.

"Daddy says that he's a rebel soldier," Elizabeth announced.

Dear God, Bathsheba thought.

"And what a mess he is. He's in the kitchen. Come and see."

It was bad enough having lodgers in the house whenever Joshua needed ready cash, which was often now that dealing in English goods, his specialty, was considered treasonous. Bathsheba resented the intrusion of these passing strangers, turning the household upside down, displacing the children from their chamber to mats down in the kitchen. And now to have Joshua drag in some puking rebel soldier was just too much. To hell with both of them! "So where is your father?"

"Don't know. He went off. To Cooley's, maybe?"

"And Baby Bath? Who's taking care of her?"

"We left her with the sick man." Elizabeth lowered her eyes.

Bathsheba coughed as she inhaled the fine grey particles that plumed up as she dragged the bag of flour across the threshold to the pantry. Elizabeth and Josh tagged along behind, glancing at each other nervously.

The stranger was slouched at the kitchen table, staring at the fire, unable to respond to Baby Bath, who was trying to show him her cloth book of ABCs. Bathsheba looked the young man over with a steely eye. Elizabeth was right, the soldier was a mess. Not much more than a child, Bathsheba thought, barely in his teens. Fie on General Washington and his regiments of boys! One sleeve of his jacket was torn from the elbow to the wrist, and half the stitching on his boots was gone. He was perilously thin, and his eyes were fever-bright. She wondered if the tangled ropes of hair that reached down to his shoulders were blond beneath the filth. Lice, too, she thought.

She snatched her little girl away and stood looking out the window, considering what to do. The sky was clouding over, and snow was in the offing. The last thing in the world she wanted was a rebel in the house, but she couldn't turn him out on a night like this. "What's your name?" she asked. "Where from?" Her voice was sharp.

"Ezra," Baby Bath announced as she struggled to escape her mother's arms.

The stranger smiled and extended a lank hand, but he faltered when he started to get up. "I was with General Washington at Trenton, then at Princeton."

"Sit down." She couldn't have him keeling over in a faint. Nor could she stand by and watch him gaze into the fire and die. She put some dried herbs in a pot and added steaming water. "This will have to do," she said. "It's the fault of you and your ilk that I've not got a single leaf of honest tea." She handed him the cup. "Let's hope this gives you strength to wash." She ordered Elizabeth to bring a cloth and bowl. "If you weren't bone-thin, you'd be about my husband's size," she said and sent Elizabeth to Joshua's chest for clean linen and a shirt.

Clumsy from his illness, Ezra knocked the washbowl to the floor. "I'm sorry, ma'am, I'm so sorry." He tried to get up to help, but he couldn't make it, and fell back, helpless, staring at the rivulet running from the shards across a wide pine board onto the hearth. It's clear that this soldier cannot cope, Bathsheba thought as she mopped up.

She removed his stinking clothes and threw them on the back logs of the fire. What a waste, she thought, as she washed his face and sponged his body clean. What a waste that a boy should be reduced to skin and bones, all because the country has gone mad. She could see he was exhausted, but that didn't stop her from working strong lye soap into his hair, then rinsing it with vinegar and water. "We can't have vermin in this house," she told the children, watching silent and wide-eyed.

As she helped the stranger dress, her eyes met his, and she was touched by the depth of gratitude she saw. "Maybe some food will help," she said. She stirred the contents of the iron pot simmering on the trammel, and poured a ladleful of soup into a pewter bowl. But the soldier shook his head. "You've got to eat!" She really didn't mean to sound so harsh. "You can't improve unless you take some nourishment." She fed him several spoonfuls, but he could not force down the rest. Annoyed, she spread a blanket on the floor in the corner by the pantry. "Mind, stay away from him," she told the children as she drew a bed-rug over him. "He's vile with disease."

As the night wore on, the stranger tossed and groaned, but Bathsheba did not go to him. She stoked the fire frequently, however, to make sure that he was warm. She was dozing when Joshua returned and, as usual, ignored her and started towards the stairs. She was quick to block his way.

"Explain yourself!" She pointed to the sleeping invalid. "What can you be thinking of?"

"You'd have me let him die? Cooley and I hauled him from a ditch beside the road down near the tavern. Everyone was watching. The neighbors know he's here, and they have an eye on you, so treat him well. Don't let your politics diminish your humanity."

Humanity! Joshua, acting like a saint in public, while saddling her in private with the dirty work. Joshua, the ideal citizen!

The next day Ezra was delirious, and his hacking cough produced a bloody phlegm. He asked for water constantly, and complained of chest pains and an aching back. Symptoms of lung fever. Years ago Bathsheba had watched her mother nurse a stable boy afflicted with that sickness, and she knew it could be fatal. But possibly, if she could remember what to do, she might be able to pull this soldier through.

She felt Ezra's racing pulse, and remembered her mother saying that lung fever overworks the heart. She chose digitalis from her store of medicines, but it seemingly had no effect. He frequently cried out, re-living some horror of the battlefield, his closest comrade shattered by a cannon ball, fragments of his body, streaming blood, hurled against an evening sky. At other times he wept or prayed. He has been frightened to the core, Bathsheba thought as she watched him hovering on the edge. She wished that somehow, sometime in the past, she had learned to pray.

Then, near midnight on the fourth day, she noticed that Ezra's face was no longer scarlet. She felt his forehead, it was cool.

103

During the weeks of his recovery, Ezra often talked about his past. He was the youngest of a family of seventeen, with only five brothers and three sisters still alive. His parents were God-fearing, and with Harvard College and the ministry in mind for him, they arranged that he be tutored by their pastor. "You'd like my family," Ezra told Bathsheba. "Sometimes I cry from missing them. They are kind, like you."

Bathsheba broke into a smile that was almost girlish, shy. "Thank you," she said. She wanted to be kind.

But for all his parents' hopes for him, Ezra's heart wasn't in his studies, and the war gave him an out. At fourteen, he joined the town militia and was off, first to Lexington and Concord, then to Bunker's Hill. Later, in the spring of '76, after Washington had flushed the British out of Boston, Ezra learned to beat the drum and soon was setting the pace for a regiment of farmers, shop-keepers, and boys marching behind the General to New York.

"There the Brits outnumbered us," he told Bathsheba. "Besides, we weren't a proper army, all of us in rags. As for firearms, everybody brought his own if he was lucky enough to have one, and there was never enough ammunition. And the victuals ..." Ezra scowled and rolled his eyes. "The rumors that you've heard are true," he said. "Troops deserted right and left, sometimes entire companies." Not Ezra, though.

Over and over he told her about his feats of bravery until she finally stopped him. When she made it clear she doubted that a soldier twice his age could manage all the exploits he described, he changed his tune. She could see he was just trying to amuse her, as when he played the mimic, his best interpretation being Mrs Stratten scolding Jesse for not scouring out the milk room to her satisfaction. And, as he convalesced, he entertained the children too, describing battle scenes to Little Josh and charming Elizabeth with stories about sea gulls and fishing boats, storms and sunny, sandy afternoons near his home in Ipswich. He promised he would take her there someday. He helped Baby Bath build castles with her blocks, and kept her out of mischief by reciting nursery rhymes.

His boyish, easy-going manner relaxed Bathsheba. It was obvious to her that he adored her in his adolescent way, and, yes, she was fond of him as well. He was nice to have around, a good companion. On warm spring days they would walk together through the meadows bright with dandelions and buttercups. Sometimes Elizabeth went along. Moreover, his presence somehow kept Joshua at bay. He doesn't want Ezra to see him as he really is, Bathsheba thought.

Reuben Olds sat gossiping with Joshua over a glass of stout at Cooley's. "I saw your wife walking in the woods with that young soldier staying at your place," Olds said. "He picked a bunch of violets for her, and the way she accepted them..." He winked suggestively.

"Damn!" Joshua polished off his drink.

"Don't be too harsh," Olds called after him, then shook his head. He should have kept his mouth shut.

Joshua found Bathsheba in the sitting room helping Elizabeth with French verbs. "Slut!"

Elizabeth snatched up her copybook and fled.

Speechless, Bathsheba tilted back her head and clenched her fists.

"Treasonous whore, daughter of a sonofabitch. Bitch!" His face was distorted, his voice savage.

"So you believe everything you hear against me, probably spread tales yourself." She paced, thrashing. "As a wronged husband, then, why don't you beat me in town square. It's your right, your duty, even. Oh, no! You'd not do that. It would change how people think of you! You are a coward, Joshua. Not only in the way you deal with me, not only that. This country is being torn to pieces, and what do you do? Drink! I wish to God you'd drink yourself to death! Go ahead. Do that!" She paused, breathless, then hurled the thought away. "A good idea, but it would take too long."

He lowered his head and squinted at her, an animal on attack. "All Brookfield knows that you and Ross are lovers. You seduced him. Everybody knows. You'll pay."

"Cuckolded husband in a rage," she mocked. "Go ahead, believe what you wish. But we'll see. We'll see who will pay."

Later, recovered from her outburst, Bathsheba quietly told Ezra he must leave, and why.

"Would they were true, his allegations." Ezra sounded almost wistful. "I'll go, but if I get a chance, I will return. Never fear. I'll be careful, for both your sake and mine."

From the window in the sitting room, she watched him walk away, down the road to Worcester, carrying his knapsack packed with the necessities she'd given him for his long trek home. She would miss him, oh, she would miss him terribly, alone again with Joshua.

Chapter 22

October, 1777

The Convention Troops came through Brookfield, right past the Spooner house, on their way to Boston. Everybody knew that they were prisoners of war, even though British General John Burgoyne insisted on calling the terms of his surrender a "Convention." That way, at least in his mind, it was less of a humiliation and just a simple international agreement.

Elated by the American victory, the citizens of Brookfield lined up along the road to watch. The spectacle went on for hours, well over five thousand British troops on the march—Englishmen and Scots, Canadians and Hessian mercenaries, along with many wives and other less legitimate companions.

The event was colorful, the English and Scots in their red coats, the Hessians in their blue. Their American guards from the New York units also wore blue uniforms, lined with white and embellished with gold buttons. By contrast, those from Massachusetts looked drab in their homespun farmer's garb. Burgoyne's carriage, painted royal blue and decorated with gold leaf, was drawn by two white horses. Thirty green and yellow wagons followed, carrying his personal possessions. But his mistress' chaise was missing. The gossips had it right that until the final battle, he'd dined with her each evening at a damask-covered table set with silver plate and glasses of champagne. But when the fighting escalated toward the end, he sent her back to Canada.

Orders shouted by the guards mingled with the clatter of the carts and wagons of artillery. Pigs and cattle of the commissariat added to the din, as did wild beasts, brought along by Hessians, who had a penchant for collecting them. One prisoner was leading a small black bear, and another had a fawn. A young raccoon, riding on a private's shoulder, brought cheers from the children in the crowd. Some circus, Bathsheba thought, as she watched from a window in the sitting room.

The retreat was far from disciplined, and in the uproar and confusion, it was easy for prisoners to escape, especially at night. Over the next few days they emerged from their hiding places all along the route and began to roam the countryside in search of work and food. One such was Alexander Cummings, a Scot who appeared at Spooner's door one brisk November morning. Joshua looked him over. "Maybe I could use you for a day or two," he said. "In exchange for board and a place to sleep out in the barn, nothing more."

Bathsheba had half expected to see Ezra among the soldiers serving as guards of the defeated English troops. She knew that he had re-enlisted, for he'd stopped by one evening in July on his way to join the American forces in Vermont. "To avenge my brother's death from a Redcoat's bayonet at Fort Ticonderoga," he had explained.

But Ezra did not come down with the Convention Troops, nor did he come soon after, not till mid-December. "Is it all right for me to come inside?" he asked.

"Yes!" She accepted his embrace. "Joshua's in Boston. At least I think that's where he is."

Ezra greeted Mrs Stratten, ironing near the fire.

Then, almost in unison, both women spoke, asking where he'd been these many months."

"Mrs Spooner has been fretting, worrying," Mrs Stratten said. "She'd just about decided you'd been killed."

"I almost was, in the battle at Freeman's Farm. A bullet in my chest laid me low for months."

He looks older, Bathsheba thought. He's been through a lot.

"I've left the army, this time for good. I'm on my way back home. But I'd like to catch my breath. It's a long walk from Saratoga to the coast." He turned to Mrs Stratten. "Maybe I could lodge a day or two with you?"

"Aye. I like your company well enough."

Later, after Mrs Stratten had served dinner, Ezra suggested that Bathsheba join him for an outing the next day.

"That is not possible," she said. But, oh, she would like nothing better. "No. It's just not possible."

"Not even a few hours?"

"Just imagine what would happen if he discovered that I'd gone away with you."

"He might die of apoplexy, and that wouldn't be so bad."

"If you went, and Mr Spooner should come back while you were gone, I'd cover for you somehow," Mrs Stratten offered.

"It's quite impossible." Then, after a long pause, "Anyway, neither of us has a horse."

"Well, there's always Captain Weldon. Ten to one, he'll let you take a couple of his mares." Mrs Stratten turned to Ezra. "Slip him a Continental. You must have earned a few for all that fighting."

Ezra laughed at her. "Come now! You know as well as I do that a Continental isn't worth a damn."

Bathsheba still resisted. As attractive as a day away from Brookfield seemed, it wasn't worth the risk.

"You love to ride," Ezra coaxed. "And it looks as if the weather will be fair. An occasional get-away is not a sin, you know."

No, it wasn't.

Just as Mrs. Stratten had predicted, everything was easily arranged, and the next morning Ezra and Bathsheba took off for New Braintree. Uncle John immediately made Ezra feel at home. While Bathsheba was tending to the horses, he took the young man by the hand and led him to the parlor. "She'll take forever," he said. "No one matches Bathshua when it comes to horses. She wrote me about Bridie, that she no longer has the mare, no explanation. It's strange. It has made me wonder, she so loved that horse."

"Yes. She sometimes mentions Bridie, always with sadness. I've detected anger, too."

"Ah, well… Let me show you something while she's gone."

On the table were two disks. About eight inches in diameter, one was made of sealing wax, the other copper with a wooden handle at its center. John rubbed the wax piece with a rabbit's pelt, round and round, as fast as he was able, singing to himself and sending wisps of fur across the kitchen floor. When he was satisfied that he had rubbed enough, he placed the metal on the wax. He waited, eyes lowered, hands together, as if in prayer. After several seconds, he touched the upper surface of the copper, and then, grasping its handle with ritual precision, he removed it from the wax. "Now," he said to Ezra, "bring your finger to it, slowly."

Ezra looked at John uncertainly, but did as he was told. An instant later, a spark shot through the air from the disk to Ezra's hand. He jumped, then laughed. John clapped and danced around the table, sat down and scribbled in his notebook. "Do it again?" he asked.

Ezra declined.

John changed the subject. "Tell me, how is it you know Shua?"

He listened thoughtfully. "And her husband?" he asked. "How did he feel about her nursing you?"

"In the end, he took things all wrong. I left. I come back now and then, but very carefully."

"Can you tell me more?" John's sincerity invited confidence.

"Mr Spooner is poison. Did you notice how pale she is?"

"You mean he's poisoning her?!"

"Not arsenic, I think, but something worse."

John heard Bathsheba coming and quickly changed the subject. "You must try my cider, Shua," he announced. "The apples came from the tree my father, your Reverend Granddaddy gave me long ago." He smiled, as if lost in pleasant thoughts. "A good man. His parishioners loved and honored him until the day he died. I did too." He took down a pewter pitcher from an open shelf and hurried to the keg outside the kitchen door.

"It's gone a trifle hard," he said when he returned. "So much the better!" He filled three mugs with the tawny, frothing beverage, and, after offering soda crackers to his guests, he ventured to ask, "What happened to your Bridie?"

Bathsheba's expression warned him not to question further. "I don't have her any more," was all she said, and then quickly gave a rundown on the children, not mentioning Joshua. "Brother Timothy and Mama are having a hard time," she added.

"Everyone is having a hard time." John paused, with a glance that told her he was thinking especially about her. He shook his head. "Everyone," he repeated. "I feel low whenever I'm in Hardwick and go by your father's place. It's so changed from what it was before the war, the buildings and the orchards all run down, no animals about. No laughter anywhere."

It was after noon by the time Ezra and Bathsheba left. The sky had filled with clouds, and frost was in the air. They cantered to keep warm, but as they neared a tavern on the lonely shortcut leading through North Parish, Bathsheba slowed her horse. Although the place appeared to be abandoned, a sign above the door promised the best food and drink in Worcester County.

"The cold air and the exercise have made me hungry," she told Ezra. And I'm in no hurry to get home, she thought. This day with Ezra and Uncle John, away from Joshua's house, seemed like a day in heaven.

The short, stocky man who met them at the bar looked them over with a knowing smile. He's wondering if we're lovers, Bathsheba thought. Had Brookfield gossip reached his ears?

"Would you like our little dining room upstairs?" he asked.

Bathsheba shook her head.

"Why not?" Ezra demanded.

Yes, why not?

The innkeeper chose a taper from the box beside the hearth and lit the candle in a chamberstick. "The stairway ain't well lit," he warned.

"Don't hit your heads on them two fire buckets hanging from the risers."

The room was small, furnished with three Windsor chairs and a table by the fire. The flames were reflected in a gold-framed mirror embellished at the top with a painting of Europa and a handsome, gentle-looking bull. Like Papa's favorite bull, Bathsheba thought. The proprietor threw a large log on the fire. "I'll send up my lass to take your order, sir," he said. "I'll have her bring some wine."

Bathsheba removed her cape and settled back. Her eyes lingered on the tall clock in the corner, with the changing phases of the moon painted on its face, almost exactly like the one Nathan so admired in the best parlor of the house in Hardwick. Those far off times seemed now like something she had read about in someone else's life.

"I've enjoyed the day," she said after they had eaten. "I'm glad that you insisted."

She ran her finger around the rim of her Madeira glass as she listened to the lazy crackle of the fire. Through the window she could see giant snowflakes falling like a silent curtain, shutting out the world. She remembered a winter day when she was in her teens, she and Nathan walking in her father's deer park, then stopping awhile to build a snowman. How close we were, she thought.

Lost in her reverie, she started when Ezra spoke. "You know," he said, "I think I would do anything for you." His eyes worshiped her.

He's misinterpreting my mood, she thought and reached for her cape. Then, in a brisk tone, "Come. We must make it back to Brookfield before dark."

Chapter 23

Ezra paid another visit six weeks later, on the frigid evening of February first. "I saw Joshua's horse outside Cooley's Tavern," he said. "So I figured that the coast was clear for awhile at least." He explained that he had been in Worcester, working for an elderly acquaintance of his father. "And being so near, I had to see you, if only for a minute, before going back to Ipswich." He asked about the children.

She said they were in bed. Her voice was flat, and she had an odd, almost vacant look. With nervous fingers she brushed back untidy strands of hair.

Ezra studied her a moment. "Whatever is the matter?"

She could tell that he was shocked by her appearance. Perhaps she should make an effort to explain. But then again, why bother? It would sound excessive to say that the weeks since she'd seen him last had proved too much for her, that her vitality had been sapped, drained by the monotony of winter storms, her isolation, and, most of all, by Joshua's abuse, which sometimes now was physical. She slept a lot.

She stooped down to the wood box for a log to feed the fire, and her heavy shawl snagged on a piece of bark. She let it fall.

"How thin you are," Ezra murmured. "How changed."

"Am I?" What difference did it make.

Ezra came closer and reached out.

So were they standing, side by side, her shawl apparently cast off, when Joshua burst in, looming in the doorway in his great black coat and tricorn hat. The candle on the table flickered in the draft and died.

Rocking on his heels, he squinted through the firelight at Ross, then lurched a little nearer. "Got your baby prick up for her? Well, be my guest. Right here on the floor. Why not?" He stank of rum.

Bathsheba started to back off. He grabbed her by both wrists. She twisted, kicked, spat in his face. He whipped her around and took a stand behind her, offering her to Ezra, who was inching toward the door with dread and hatred in his eyes. "What's the matter?" Joshua taunted. "You aren't interested any more? It's my turn, then?"

Bathsheba's strength surged, fed by hate. She would stop him, maim him, kill him! She wrenched free of Joshua and seized the fire tongs.

But before she could bring them down on him, he wrested them away. He steered her, fighting, through the dark front hall and up the stairs, and when they reached the bed, he pressed her down. She clawed at him. He slammed a pillow on her face. She tore at it. He forced her over and grabbed his mermaid pipe, left on the candle stand. Then torture, jabbing, tearing her apart, pain more than she could bear, on and on until he was sufficiently aroused. He threw her on her back, then down and down again until he finished and cast her off.

She lay still as death, blood seeping out. She felt as if she'd died but was not dead. Not dead enough, she thought, wishing she could no longer think or feel or smell. As she smoldered there, her dark thoughts hardened forever against this man she lived with, the father of her children, who had used her in this monstrous way.

Much later, she became aware that dawn was slanting across the bed and Ezra was standing near. "He's gone, but he'll be back," he said. "I could hear a lot, but when he came downstairs, he acted as if nothing at all unusual had happened. He got water from the well and washed his bloody, murky pipe, wiped it dry, and then, by God, he filled it and sat down to smoke. By some evil transformation, he took on the part of being my friend, asking me to go with him to Princeton for a week to inspect some land he said your father gave him."

"Don't go!"

"I know. You're right. He no doubt plans to kill me. But I agreed. I'll get him before he has a chance at me. I found some *aqua fortis* in your cabinet. I'll dose his grog. I'll make it look as if he had a failure of the heart. We'll leave within the hour."

"It won't work. Its bitter taste will warn him. Don't get mixed up in this, believe me, it will undo you. You're too young."

Ezra wasn't listening. "One way or another, I'll get rid of him. Shall I bring the body back?"

Chapter 24

When she was certain that Joshua and Ezra had departed, Bathsheba crawled from her blood-stained bed, cleansed herself and put on fresh linen and clean clothes. Pain knifed down her back, between her legs. She stopped by the children's chamber, filled with apprehension that they might have been wakened in the night and heard. But they looked undisturbed, innocent, slumbering in their cots.

The back stairs were torture. She crept across the kitchen, whispering thanks to Ezra—it must have been Ezra—for leaving a blazing fire. She warmed her hands and glanced around the room. Every detail seemed like something it was not—the herbs and onions hanging from the summer beam were felons dangling from their gallows, dim corners were filled with demons, quivering shadows everywhere.

Mrs Stratten found Bathsheba huddled by the fire. "Law, ma'am," she said. "You don't look yourself."

"I am unwell." Grey as death. "Please take the children home with you. I'm not fit to give them proper care right now. I'll send word by Jesse when I'm better. A day or so."

Mrs Stratten stepped back to consider. "I don't know, ma'am, you oughtn't to be by yourself."

"Go! Go and take the children."

Mrs Stratten's expression bordered on alarm. Never before had Mrs Spooner ordered her like that, giving such an unmistakable command.

"Please."

Mrs Stratten shook her head and went upstairs. "I don't like the look of it at all," she mumbled as she packed a duffel bag with a few things for the children.

Throughout the endless hours that followed, Bathsheba wrestled with her thoughts. She could no longer live with Joshua, with hate and fear, and she repeatedly came to the conclusion that there was only one way to escape. But over and over she backed off, alarmed that she even could consider such a thing. She detested violence and flaunting of the law. Yet, in a case like this, a higher law applied—didn't it? Could she do it? And, if she did, could she abide herself after he was buried? Round and round, down and down, until finally, desperate for sleep, she searched her cabinet for relief, swallowed as much thick poppy syrup as she dared, and lay down in the borning room.

Panic shot through her dream. Joshua appeared before her dying, clawing air, white arsenic and spittle trailing from his lips. She cried out for Ezra, but her voice was soundless, and Ezra wasn't there, nor was Joshua dead, just waiting.

Then, out of nowhere, the Devil materialized, trailing a sulfurous cloud and smiling. Strands of jet-black hair curled puckishly around his polished ivory horns.

"What are your plans?" he asked.

"I could flee and take my children to my mother's house."

The Devil shook his head. "Oh, but Mr S would find you in an instant and bring you back and punish you in such a way you would not want to live. You belong to him, by law, to do with as he pleases." He whirled his huge black cape to display its crimson lining and his sleek black leather suit. "If you are so foolish as to insist on running from your problem," he continued, "you must go miles and miles away, to another colony, hide somewhere, and, without money, which you do not have, that would be impossible, now wouldn't it? Besides, such a course of action would bring deprivation to your children. Further, I remind you, that you, Bathsheba Ruggles, could not live in hiding, it's against your nature."

117

He knows me, she thought, he sees things clearly. Maybe she could trust him. "Should I consider divorce?" she asked, as a sort of test to which she already knew the answer.

The Devil picked up Joshua's mermaid pipe, examined it, and grinned. "Hmm. A divorce granted to a Tory woman by a rebel court? A laughable idea. Your father might have helped in better days, he knew how to deal with the law, but even in the best of times, adultery is the only charge the courts would listen to. If you so charged—and I know you'd like to—Mr S would be sure to countercharge, pointing to Ezra as your lover. He would drag you through shame and public beatings, and in the end, his word, not yours, would be accepted."

"It's hopeless, then."

"Oh, there is a way. I'm sure you know that there's a way. I've watched you thinking on it." He stood tall, one cloven foot thrust slightly forward, then raised his beautiful forked tail and placed it on his shoulder. He wore it handsomely and looked all-knowing and majestic. "I have it in my power to help." His smile was tempting. "You must admit you made a big mistake. You should have given Ezra arsenic for the trip. You were foolish to have tried to protect the lad. But you lost your opportunity, so let's move on. Pay me due respect, and I will guide you. Keep in mind that the man you chose to marry has no right to live, and when the time comes, I'll be there."

Bathsheba awakened with a start to find Mrs Stratten watching over her. "The children?" she asked. "Something's wrong."

"Right now they're with their cousins at your sister Martha's place. Nothing's wrong with them. But Jesse came to tell me he thought things were bad with you."

"They were. I think I'm better now." She sat up and peered out the window. "Snow-clouds," she said. She stared into the looking glass, hardly recognizing the disheveled image that stared back, disfigured further by a crack that ran across the mirror.

Mrs Stratten helped her wash and dress and told her she must eat. "I brought some bread, fresh baked." She cut thick slices and laid them out with cheese. "I really ought to stay, keep you company and tidy up the place." She took measure of the clouds. "My bones tell me, though, that we're in for quite a storm. It wouldn't do to be snowbound here. I can't leave the children with your sister for who knows how long." She set a pot of coffee on a grate. "I'd best get home. Be sure you eat, now, ma'am."

Alex Cummings let himself into the kitchen without so much as knocking. Although hired by Joshua months ago "for only a few days," he was still living in the barn, ever since he deserted ·the Convention Troops. It was folly, Bathsheba thought, for Joshua to allow him to stay on. Alex wasn't worth it, he did next to nothing in return. Besides, she did not like him, and she sensed he felt the same regarding her.

"Excuse me, ma'am," he said. "Down at Cooley's just now, I met an old comrade from the Canadian campaign. Happens he's a fellow countryman from Edinburgh. He and a chum of his are looking for a place, what with the storm that's coming on. I told them I'd inquire if it's all right for them to share the barn with me."

"I'm surprised you bother to ask."

"Well, ma'am, I thought you might be willing to, well, maybe also offer them a bite to eat?"

So that's it. She hesitated. Still, these men were soldiers who had served the British cause. There was enough food in the pantry, and it might help to have someone to dine with, someone to divert her mind, someone who would take her at face value, no questions asked. Moreover, she felt reckless. "Tell them to come along," she said.

She held out her hand in greeting. Tall and swarthy with an air of crafty, quick intelligence, the Scot tilted back his head and grinned. He introduced himself as Sergeant James Buchanan. "And this fellow here is Private William Brooks." A stocky man of powerful build, whose puffy face was circled by a wide white scar that ran beneath his chin from ear to ear.

"You're from the Convention Troops?" She motioned them to have a seat.

119

Buchanan said they were. He looked around and smiled. "A lot better here than in some flea-coop of a tavern, eh Brooks?"

She guessed that they would think themselves well off if they had a cup of coffee in the kitchen, but that didn't fit her mood. This jaunty Scot sparked her old penchant for adventure, and, in an offhand way, as if it were her custom, she asked Alex please to set the table in the sitting room. He looked astounded and Brooks looked befuddled, but Buchanan's eyes were lively with anticipation. He grinned at his good luck.

"Brooks here and I have been together quite awhile," he said in answer to Bathsheba's questions. "He comes from England. The both of us got caught up in the army, and chanced to be in Charlestown when that bleedin' mess began at Bunker's Hill."

Bathsheba liked the way Buchanan talked, his confidence, his brogue.

"Brooks and me," the Scot was going on, "we stuck together and finally wound up with Burgoyne."

Bathsheba studied Brooks. He hadn't said a word since he came in, and she wondered if perhaps he couldn't talk. Buchanan seemed to read her mind. "Brooks don't say much," he said. "He's so ugly no one fancies striking up a conversation. You're wondering, perhaps, about the scar? A brother of a man he killed in London tried to take revenge, but didn't cut quite deep enough for thorough satisfaction. It happened a long time ago. After that, Billie thought it best to get away, and the army seemed like a good bet." Brooks sat staring at his boots. "Right now," Buchanan added, "we're on our way to Springfield to try to find some work. Then maybe Canada, high up, where there's no fuckin' war."

He took down one of Joshua's clay pipes from the wall rack and filled it with Joshua's tobacco. "Who ever would have thought that we'd be sitting here in Brookfield, in the lap of luxury, about to feast in style with a lady." He winked at her, as he reached for Joshua's pipe tongs. She returned a shadow of a smile. He tilted back his chair and rocked on its back legs. "Like falling into a tub of butter, eh, Brooks?" But Brooks was fast asleep.

Buchanan stopped rocking and sat grinning at Bathsheba. Like the Devil, she thought. She got up, went over to the window, and for awhile watched the advancing blizzard wrestle with the trees. She should tell these scoundrels to go on their way, right now, before the storm got worse. But it already was too late, no one could go anywhere in such heavy weather. Nor did she really want them to.

"Did Alex tell you my husband is away?" she asked.

"Your husband, eh? And where is he?"

"At his potash farm in Princeton, up north of Worcester." Or maybe he would be here any minute, rushing back, trying to beat the storm—alone. She shivered and drew her shawl close around her shoulders.

Buchanan found a glass and strode across the room to Joshua's rum dispenser. "You look like you have seen a ghost," he said as he turned on the tap. "Have a little. It will do you good. Bring some color to those cheeks. ."

"I never drink."

He cocked his head, still grinning.

She reached out and took the glass.

"I assume you'll let us lodge here for the night," he said.

The storm grew worse. It was almost dark by mid-afternoon when Alex and Bathsheba sat down with the soldiers to a meal of bread and ham. They were all drawn together in a ring of candlelight, isolated from the fury of the weather. She wished that Ezra was there too, safe with them and free of Joshua. She pushed back thoughts of Nathan. He would hate to see her here like this. Then, slowly, she loosened up, partly because the rum was having its effect, but more than that because she knew that by now there was no way Joshua could suddenly appear. Let the blizzard rage!

"When you're done, come back," she said to Alex, on his way out to feed the animals. "The barn's no place for anyone to sleep tonight." Not even Alex. "There's room enough for all of you upstairs. I always use the borning room." She asked Buchanan to help Alex with the kitchen door, almost impossible to open now against the wind and bank of snow.

Later, when Alex came back in, Buchanan filled four tumblers with Joshua's rum, one each all around. He threw more logs onto the fire.

"Here," Bathsheba said, handing him a glowing taper from the hearth. "Please light the Betty lamps."

"A pleasure to be sure," he answered with mock gallantry. When he finished, he gave back the taper and stepped up close as she tried to light a candle on the narrow shelf above. But her hand was shaking, and his closeness made things worse. When he ran his hand around her waist and reached up to her breast, she froze, then dropped the taper, spun around, and slapped his face.

Buchanan reeled back and laughed. "All right, all right!" He made a gesture of surrender. "Do you think I'd be so low as to force myself on you? I just thought a caress or two might make you feel less nervous. You're awfully jittery, you know." He shrugged. "But what the hell, fact is, I have a great desire for sleep. Come on now, Brooks! Upstairs! We haven't had as good a place in months."

The next morning the blizzard was still howling, making drifts so high they blocked the light at the west windows. Buchanan was all smiles as he poured himself some coffee. He ladled out some porridge and beamed at his hostess, watching from across the room. "Nothing like a good night's sleep," he said.

She made no response. Buchanan may have slept just fine, but her sleep had been shattered by nightmares. Besides she had a headache.

"So all right." Buchanan said. "Don't look so sullen. It doesn't matter. I just thought I'd wish you a good day."

A trace of a smile rewarded his concern.

He turned his attention to necessities. "Help Alex shovel a path out to the outhouse," he ordered Brooks.

When the chores were done, the men relaxed, smoking by the kitchen fire, discussing old times and totaling up the number of Americans they'd killed.

At dinner that afternoon, Buchanan tried to draw Bathsheba out, tempting her again with rum. "Hair of the dog that bit you," he quipped. "Come now, don't worry. I promise I'll make no more passes. But you know it wouldn't hurt to talk, might do you good."

Maybe he was right. It's odd, she thought, how sometimes one can feel easy with a stranger, tell things one wouldn't dream of telling a sister or a friend. She sipped from the glass he'd given her and began to feel hazy, warm. "My husband and I, we don't agree," she ventured.

"So?" Buchanan's steady gaze invited her to keep on talking. "I'm a sympathetic man, you know," he said

For three days the storm continued, beating down the western hills into the valleys, by far the worst in anybody's memory, and when at last the weather cleared, the task of digging out was daunting. "It will be at least a couple of days before the road is passable," Buchanan said at supper. "So we might as well enjoy our time together, right?" He filled glasses for himself and Brooks and Alex, then tilted the bottle toward Bathsheba with a glance that challenged her to join them.

He's good company, she thought, makes one forget, like the travelers who'd stopped by while the celebration boomed in Hinkley's meadow, years ago, before the real trouble started. But Buchanan was infinitely more interesting. There was something exciting about him, something in the way he talked, his insolence, his nonchalance.

"We'll be leaving as soon as we can make it," he said. "I know you'll miss us, especially Brooks."

Bathsheba grimaced.

"Well, cheer up. We'll come back some day. Besides, it won't be long before you'll have your husband home again."

Bathsheba drew in her breath, and Buchanan leaned forward, at attention. Abandoning all caution, she said she could no longer live with Mr Spooner. She told about the *aqua fortis*, omitting any mention of the incident that led to it. "It won't work, of course. My husband's not a fool. He wouldn't drink the stuff."

"Interesting," Buchanan said, nodding thoughtfully.

Interesting! This sergeant seemed to view premeditated murder as some kind of game. But why should that surprise her? He bragged all the time about all those Americans he'd slaughtered on the battlefield. It was all the same to him. "You have no idea how bad my situation is," she said.

"Well, I can guess. You got yourself hitched up with this bastard and now you're having trouble finding a way out."

"Please don't." He made it sound so low, so crass.

"Come, come. Face facts. Look at it this way: in your case it sounds to me as if it's either you or him, and from what you've told me, the right is on your side."

Right? Wrong? Which is which?

"You know," Buchanan said, "despite the fact you look dragged out, a bit like a whipped dog, you're quite beautiful."

She turned away. The compliment was welcome; she felt wretched.

"Think it over. Don't get hung up on moral philosophy, and, remember, for a monetary consideration, we might help." He called to Brooks. "Come on, let's fight our way through drifts to Cooley's for an hour. After being cooped up here for days, I have a hankering for a little tavern atmosphere."

The following afternoon, just as Alex and the soldiers were drinking to Bathsheba's thirty-second birthday, Joshua arrived home. How hateful his appearance! Did he remember how savage he had been, how depraved? And where was Ezra? Bathsheba struggled to seem calm, she asked how his trip had been. She introduced the soldiers, spilling out the first explanation she could think of. "Sergeant Buchanan is Alex's cousin," she said. Alex's jaw dropped, but he held his tongue. "Private Brooks is the Sergeant's friend. Caught in the storm, they've been lodging here."

Joshua did not seem to take exception to their presence, and she rushed on to the more pressing question. "Where is Ezra?"

At first Joshua did not reply. He took a candle and started towards the stairs, but before he left the room he turned and withdrew from his pocket the bottle that had once contained the *aqua fortis*. He held it high, removed the stopper, and tipped it top to bottom, demonstrating it was empty. "I suppose you'll try to tell me you know nothing about this." His smile repulsed her. "Are you so naïve as to think I wouldn't turn the screw on him?" Looking steadily at Bathsheba, he hurled the bottle across the room, and it splintered on the hearth.

"You didn't dare!"

Buchanan stepped up behind her as her husband disappeared up the back stairs. "He's worse than I expected," he whispered. He turned her around to face him, touched her chin and tilted back her head, forcing her to look at him. "Don't jump to conclusions," he said. "Maybe he didn't kill the boy, but whatever he did or didn't do, we'll have to figure something. Here, have a little rum."

Her hand was shaking so, she could hardly hold the glass.

Chapter 25

Before mixing him some flip, Ephriam Cooley handed Joshua the bill for the liquor the soldiers had consumed. Reuben Olds, seated at a table by the fire, noticed a flash of anger streak across Joshua's face. "Welcome back," he said, beckoning him over. "How d'ya like those fellows up at your place?" Watching Joshua's reaction, he took a long draw on his pipe. "I ran into them myself one day when I stopped by to ask Alex to give me a hand repairing my ox yoke." He added that the soldiers had been there for a week. "Alex says they talk a lot, not always beneficial towards you."

Joshua shoved the liquor bill towards Olds, and pointed to the tab. Olds rolled his eyes. "Spooner," he said, "take my advice. Go home and kick 'em out."

Joshua looked undecided. He muttered something about feeling threatened by the soldiers, they made him feel uncomfortable—that arrogant Scot, taking over as if he owned the place, and, as for the Englishman, well, it was easy to see that he'd as soon knock a fellow down as cuss him out.

"So throw 'em out," Olds urged. "Of course, you oughta make them pay up first, but maybe it's not worth it. They could cause a lot of trouble: steal the plate, poison the horses, set the house on fire, kill anyone who happened to get in their way."

"That's just it. I don't favor the idea of getting in their way." He filled his pipe. "Why don't you come back with me? Not that I couldn't best them, I've dealt with worse. But, if they cause an ugly scene, I'd like to have a witness to back me up when I turn them in to the Committee."

Olds took his time considering. "I'm not keen on getting mixed up in this," he said. "It ain't my business, and add to that, I don't like the look of that English thug any more than you do." In the end, though, after a couple more bumpers of beer, he agreed to come.

"Send them away," Joshua told Bathsheba. "You took them in. You throw them out."

"I heard," Buchanan said before she had a chance to speak. He got up from Joshua's favorite chair. "What's eating the old bogus now?"

She gestured, indicating they should use the barn. She didn't want them off too far; she felt safer when they were around. Besides, Buchanan had all but promised help.

"Come on, Brooks," he said. "The master wants us out." He put on his coat. "But we won't abandon you," he whispered as he edged past Bathsheba to the door.

For the next few days the soldiers dodged about, back and forth from house to barn to tavern, keeping out of Joshua's way. Gossip concerning them was brisk. They were obviously a menace: Buchanan, wily; Brooks, a wild dog. They'd been seen hanging around the Brookfield magazine, and Brooks had bragged at Cooley's about their plans for blowing it to hell. Patrons nodded to each other, agreeing that the Committee ought to lock up these two foreigners; they were clearly enemies of the people.

Bathsheba got her share from the gossipmongers, too. That she was a Tory had long been enough to get the women going, but even more than that, she never stopped to mingle. She obviously thought that, because she was so beautiful and her father once had been so wealthy, she was above them. But, they whispered, the Brigadier had been brought down, now, hadn't he? And soon she would be, too. Scandal was in the air, and they'd put it to good use. Why, just think of it, Mrs Spooner taking in those British Regulars with Mr Spooner gone! A traitor, and a whore to boot!

Though Mrs Stratten had for years shared stories with the gossips, she would brook no slurs against her mistress now. It never had mattered a whit to her that Mrs Spooner was a Tory; one side in this

127

endless war was no better than the other, as far as she could tell. Besides, she had seen many things close to, and she had never for a moment forgotten Mrs Spooner's kindness to Rebecca. People misjudged the mistress, they didn't know her, they didn't know how really kind she was, how hard it was to live with Mr Spooner. Mrs Stratten hated him, despised him. And, what was worse, for all these years, she had had to keep this to herself for fear of losing her employment; a widow has to live. But now that the lines were being drawn, she had no trouble choosing sides. And when one day Jesse came to her, uncertain what to think, she set him straight about the master and Rebecca.

Time had far from dimmed Jesse's feelings for his secret sweetheart, and when he heard who'd harmed her—killed her, he insisted—it did not take him long to decide what he should do. He sought out Brooks. "Tomorrow," he told him, "early in the morning, I'm going with Spooner to the country for some oats." His tone was scheming, low. "We'll probably be coming back by noon. Lay wait for us on that lonely stretch on Mile River Road, right after Weldon's farm."

Brooks stared at him, confused.

"Don't you see? You'd have a perfect chance to do him in. Don't think I haven't heard you plotting with that Scot. Just this morning, while I was milking, I heard him say he would get the keenest pleasure helping Spooner to his grave, and you agreeing."

Brooks promised nothing, but reported to Buchanan, who shook his head. "Too risky, too much in the open, and broad daylight too." But he grinned. "No doubt about it, this Spooner sonofabitch has a knack for getting people's hackles up. I wonder what he's done to Jesse." Not that it mattered. For whatever reason, Jesse just might be of use.

So the conspirators connived, by now including Alex, who joined up more from bravado than from conviction. True, he didn't like the way that Spooner treated him, ordering him about like he was dirt. But, more than that, he didn't want to be left out. "I've been a soldier just like you, you know," he told Buchanan.

It soon became a game to think up ways of getting rid of Joshua. Out in the barn, plot after plot was hatched and then rejected: he could be attacked in bed one night, and his body thrown into the well so that it looked like he had lost his balance and fallen in while drawing water. Or Alex or Jesse—it didn't matter which—could tell him that his horse was sick and needed his attention. Then, when he came out to the barn, Brooks could attack him and throw him underneath the horse's feet, leaving the impression that the animal had trampled him to death.

Bathsheba was kept informed. "I tell you, it's like this," Buchanan said. "Brooks and I are broke, dead broke, and we've been talking. A thousand dollars or whatever's in your husband's money box of whatever currency, and we'll end your misery." She wouldn't have to do a thing, just pay.

She agonized, she knew that she should stop him, but she let things drift. Not until Buchanan demanded an advance was she jolted to reality. Impossible! She herself had nothing, and Joshua's money box was always locked, with the key always on his person. Besides, she was having second thoughts. "Leave me alone, Buchanan! For God's sake!"

By Sunday night he had lost all patience. "Indecisive wench," he muttered to Brooks. "There's no future in this mess. Those two bloody fools, Alex and Jesse, with their air brained ideas, are sure to botch things up."

"We've had enough," he told Bathsheba as he lounged in the kitchen after Joshua left for Cooley's. "We're going to leave tomorrow, early, to find some work, earn enough to start us on our way to Canada. This country be damned. Believe me, Mrs S, assisting you would give me pleasure, on my own account as well as yours. But when Brooks and I consider things cold sober, we see all too clear that it's a shaky business, and we can't afford to risk our necks for nothing, with no guarantee we'll ever see just compensation. Thanks for the food and lodging, such as it's been of late." He said goodnight, goodbye. "For better or for worse, the best of luck to you."

She should have known Buchanan would walk out on her; commitment was not his forte. Now, without him, she felt abandoned, fearful, without hope, her only refuge from Joshua the borning room, where she could close the door and lock it. But it was cold and without comfort.

Mrs Stratten stopped by every morning for an hour or so, but she didn't like to leave the children long. "A good thing, too, that they are still with me. This house is no proper place for youngsters."

No proper place for anyone. She, Bathsheba Spooner, hated it and everything about it. She felt possessed, no more connected to Bathsheba Ruggles than to a stranger in a far off foreign land centuries ago. That distant woman had been young and beautiful and kind, in love with a good man, a man much like her father. Now she, Bathsheba Spooner, was edging toward depravity much worse than her husband's. No, not worse, not even a depravity at all. No, the course she was taking was a necessity—a justified necessity.

About nine o'clock on Wednesday night, the Regulars showed up again. She saw them coming and stepped outside before they had a chance to knock. "We're on our way to Worcester and decided to drop by," Buchanan told her. "To discuss a business matter that we left unfinished."

"No."

"Not so fast. We had a little fling at honest work with a smith in Western, but the old skinflint paid us just a meal a day, not enough to keep a sparrow alive. Besides he had no files for Brooks' branch of the trade." He went on about what a fine whitesmith Brooks was. Then, "Come now, invite us in. We could do with a little warming. We know the old bogus isn't here, we waited in the barn until we saw him leave."

Bathsheba shook her head, but at the same time stepped aside.

"Work to our liking is hard to get," Buchanan said. "So we've reconsidered. If you could review your financial situation and somehow see your way to substantial compensation, we might still be at your service." He ignored Brooks' grunt. "Think it over. Meantime,

I'm sure you won't mind our sleeping in the barn. We'll leave early, before dawn. When we get to Worcester, we plan to stay at Mrs Walker's place—you know, the tavern about a mile from the Worcester-Brookfield line. That is, unless she gets mean spirited over lack of payment the last time we were there. Her daughter Mary, though, has an eye for me, and I'll ask her to arrange things in return for a kiss or two and a little evening sport."

"You wouldn't stop at anything, Buchanan, would you?"

He went over to the bread drawer, took out a loaf, and grinned. "If, after paying a little mind to our proposition, you want to discuss terms and ways and means, join us at Walker's tomorrow afternoon." He took a glass from the kitchen dresser and filled it with Joshua's rum. "A nightcap before we hit the hay!"

Bathsheba could not sleep. Over and over she reviewed her circumstances, and always concluded that her survival hinged on Joshua's demise. In the large scheme of things, there was nothing wrong with what she knew she had to do. The only real question was how to pay the soldiers. Well, there was that length of exquisite silk she had been hoarding for a dress, it would bring a handsome sum, cloth being so scarce. She probably could borrow from M'Donald, her father's lifetime friend; she knew where he lived in Worcester. And she would promise the soldiers Joshua's moneybox, everything that's in it.

Thursday morning found her bargaining again with Captain Weldon. "I'm sorry I come so often, but I must have a horse again," she said. "I've decided to go through with it."

The Captain looked disturbed. "Going to find your father, miss?" She had told him once that she thought she ought to try, she missed him so.

She helped him saddle the horse.

"Ah, miss, be careful," he warned. "Travel these days is hazardous. I wish I knew some way to help."

"You are helping, Captain, thank you. Your kindness, be assured, will save my life."

"I hope so, ma'am, but this seems to me a vast uncertain business."

Never had Bathsheba felt so out of place, so fearfully uncomfortable. She was tempted to walk out, turn back, but she had come this far, and she'd made up her mind. She found Buchanan at the bar, oozing charm. He thanked her for the cloth and the seven dollars she had borrowed from her father's friend. A sort of down payment, she explained.

The taproom was filling up with men. "I can't stay any longer," she told Buchanan. "I'm going to my sister Mary's place, the mansion on the hill." So different from this hole.

"Mind you, don't fail to come back tomorrow," Buchanan said. "To discuss the arrangement I have in mind."

"Why are you here?" Mary was obviously astounded. "Some dreadful thing has happened? The children are all right? You don't look yourself."

Mary! Dear Mary! For a moment, Bathsheba had a great desire to tell her everything, make a clean sweep, then nestle in the comfort of her sister's home, be part of her warm family. Mary would take her in, Mary would protect her. She would arrange to bring the children.

But there was too much to tell, too much shame. So spin a web of lies. She had come to Worcester to buy some smithy files at Mr Nazro's shop, as a favor for a friend who couldn't come himself. "He was too ill," she said. "Dying, maybe." She could see that Mary did not believe a word. "I'm very tired." she said.

Her sister settled her in the well-appointed guestroom, and they kissed goodnight. "Thank you," Bathsheba said. "More than I can say."

She sat before the fire, musing. The furnishings and atmosphere brought back memories of Hardwick—snug hearths in every room, her father's study crammed with books, the stables, Bridie waiting to be curried, the orchards flowering in the spring. And Nathan dropping by, bringing a wild turkey from his hunt with Richard. All gone now, replaced by shadows.

For the first time since that fateful, hateful night, Bathsheba wept.

In the adjacent chamber, Mary and her husband talked about her sister in hushed tones. "I think she's suffering from some deep disturbance," Dr John concluded. It was Mary's turn to weep.

The following afternoon, Bathsheba put on a face that was much bolder than she felt and returned to Mrs Walker's. "He's in his room," Mary Walker said in a tone of no respect. Feeling like a criminal, Bathsheba climbed the dusty unlit stairs.

Buchanan was sitting on the bed, cutting into smaller lots some white powder spread out on the candle table. He looked up. "Hello," he said. "I've been to the apothecary. So here we are. Now listen carefully." He instructed her to mix a lethal portion into Joshua's food. He promised that he and Brooks would come on Sunday night, by which time the poison should have taken full effect. For their part, they'd collect their due from Joshua's moneybox and take care of the body. "Let several days go by before reporting that your husband's missing, so we'll have time to get far away in case some lunatic decides we're suspects. As for you, stick to your story that you know nothing of your husband's whereabouts. Emphasize that he often went away without giving you a clue. That way, the incident will soon blow over."

She glared at him. This wasn't what she'd come for, this rotten plan, their asking to be paid for next to nothing, simply supplying arsenic and carting off the body. "You're mad," she said.

Buchanan eyed her critically. "What's the matter? Chickening out? Don't worry. Be careful and follow my instructions, and there should be no problem." He pointed to the packets into which he'd folded the lots of powder. "If anybody asks, tell them it's calomel for a sick kid, something innocent like that. Nobody will suspect you."

She grabbed the packets and swerved past Pru and Mary, lurking in the hallway. She seethed through the streets, on to Mary's house, directly to the privy, and threw the packets down.

It was getting dark by the time she reached Brookfield late Saturday afternoon. She returned the Captain's horse, and walked home slowly, full of apprehension. She had been to visit sister Mary, that's all she'd say if Joshua asked. Some lie about her sister being sick.

Mrs Stratten rushed out to meet her. "Ma'am, Ezra Ross is here," she said.

"Here? Now?"

"He came on the horse he'd stolen from the master, the one he rode to Princeton. Its back is hurt, and it's tethered in the woods beyond the barn, close by the stream. Ezra's in the milk room now, not wanting Mr Spooner to discover him."

"You're still alive, not hurt!" She embraced him.

"I'm hiding here until I have a chance at him with these." He took a brace of pistols from his bag. "I failed with the poison. He found me out, but I escaped." He held up the guns. "But I'll win this time. Oh, yes, I'll win."

"Put them away!" her voice was sharp, insistent. Ezra was too young, too good a soul for games like this.

Chapter 26

Sunday morning was heavy with foreboding, Joshua sleeping off an overdose of rum, Ross still in hiding, a high wind and angry sky. Something dreadful surely lay ahead. The Regulars would arrive, expecting to find Joshua dead, and then what? She shuddered as she forced her way against the wind, obsessed with the conviction that she must see her children before it was too late.

They welcomed her politely, no hugs, no kisses.

"Did you come to take us home?" Josh asked. "Do we have to go?"

"Not now, soon, though, maybe a day or so." It didn't matter what she said as long as it covered up the truth.

"No rush," Elizabeth said. "We like it here, with cousins close. We see them every day."

Baby Bath put on a pout. "There's no fun at our house, not when Papa's there. I wish I wasn't s'posed to love him."

Mrs Stratten had prepared a dinner of pork pie and applesauce, to be topped off with hasty pudding. "I'd be honored if you'd sit down with us," she said. "You look a little wan. Did you have a pleasant visit with your sister?"

"She has a lovely home." But the thoughts that came to mind were not of sister Mary or her house, but of dirty stairs, a dirty room, Buchanan and the powder. She put down her saucerful of tea and clasped her hands together to stop their shaking.

Mrs Stratten looked perplexed. "You know, ma'am, you should go more often to your sister's place, enjoy her family. You've frequently have told me how much you love her husband's beautiful estate."

"Yes, well…" But it wasn't the house and well groomed grounds she was recalling; it was Buchanan repeating that he and Brooks would come to Brookfield and take away the body and the money. "I've had word that the Regulars might be coming back," she said. "Before the day is out."

"Law, ma'am, that's not good news." Mrs Stratten got up to clear the table. "Not good at all."

Bathsheba rose to help. "The thought of them unsettles me. Could you walk home with me, keep me company a while? The children won't be needing you. They've already made it clear that they want to spend the evening with their cousins."

The wind had died and the air was ominously still. The only sound was the crackling of the ice-filled ruts beneath the women's feet. As they neared the Spooner house, Mrs Stratten said she thought the soldiers already had arrived. "I just caught a glimpse of someone with Brooks's build dodging around out by the well," she said.

Bathsheba found the Regulars with Alex in the barn. She took Buchanan aside and confessed about the poison. "He's at Cooley's now, I guess."

Buchanan exploded. "So you've left it up to us! By God, you sicken me! There's no choice now but to let Brooks loose to put an end to this charade, then clear out with the money, Brooks and me."

There is no stopping them, not now. They're drunk enough to go through with it this time. Drunk enough that, if she dared to intervene—she wouldn't—but if she did, she probably would end up dead herself. She rushed on to tell Buchanan about Ezra and the pistols.

He thundered back at her. "Trying to upstage us, cash in on the take! Where is the bastard?" He went directly to the milk room. "Pleased to meet you," he sneered. "I've heard you can't stand the Old Bogus, either. The pistols, I can tell you, though, are out. Even an adolescent fool should be capable of figuring that gunshots would attract a flock of nosey neighbors. My buddy, Brooks, can do it with a quiet thud. Stick around and see." He hauled Ezra to the sitting room to join the others, and announced that he was taking charge. "Set out a bite to eat," he ordered Mrs Stratten.

She looked to Bathsheba for assent, did his bidding, then retreated to the barn with a hamperful of food. "I'll eat out here with you," she said to Alex. "There's trouble brewing in the house. It's no place for a Christian soul to tarry."

The sitting room was dark, save for the fitful fire and pale light from the rising moon. "No candles," Buchanan ordered. "This isn't going to be a stage production."

He served more rum. "To take the edge off." He stationed Brooks near the kitchen door, ready to lunge out, and he posted Bathsheba at the window with the best view of the road, Ross beside her. They all waited, silent, every minute crawling. The ticking of the clock was like a muted dirge. The sudden laughter of a group of neighbors passing on the road sounded like the Devil's cackle. The clock struck nine. How long? All night this would go on, a drunken dream.

Then there he was, approaching like a black ghost in the moonlight.

Bathsheba froze.

Buchanan signaled Brooks.

A monstrous thud, a choked-off scream, the crack of bones against the granite threshold.

Bathsheba's mind went black.

After the departure of the Regulars and Ross, she stood alone in the middle of the sitting room. The air was pungent, the stench rising from the smoldering breeches on the hearth. A few coins lay scattered on the floor near Joshua's broken moneybox. Brooks' dirty, blood-stained handkerchief was on the chair. Get rid of it!

The candle on the candle stand was guttering, the fire going out. She went into the kitchen, and closed the door behind her. She must shut up the sitting room forever, seal it off. Mrs Stratten, hunched on a stool before the fire, looked up from the family Bible with frightened eyes. Bathsheba knelt beside her. "You were a witness?"

"No, ma'am, I did not see the worst of it. From the moment you and I got here, I had the queerest feeling. A bad omen, I was sure, them Regulars coming like two devils on the Lord's Day, that Brooks wild in his liquor and the Sergeant ordering everyone about. I was frighted, ma'am, and I went out to be with Alex. But, ma'am, well, you were here, you must know what happened."

Bathsheba shook her head, she didn't know. She must have been taken with some violent delirium. Yes, that was it. Except that she could not escape two certainties: Joshua was dead, and she was not sorry. She stared into the fire, blazing hellfire. She clung to Mrs Stratten. "Don't go."

"You are in dreadful need, I know. But consider, ma'am, the children need me more than you do."

After Mrs Stratten left, Bathsheba lit every candle she could find, but the night refused to be pushed back. When at last the moon went down and dark turned into morning grey, she ran out barefoot towards the well, drawn to it by her need to know. The disjointed images that kept assaulting her were surely nothing but remnants of recurring nightmares. Yet, as she neared the well curb, she could not deny the bloodstains in the snow. She knelt down and buried them with trembling hands.

Shuddering from cold and fear, she looked up to find Alex watching her, and she said the first thing she could think of. "Take the horse and go to Cooley's. Hurry! Ask for Mr Spooner. Tell Mr Cooley that he's missing."

Alex looked appalled. "You're telling me you really don't know where he is?" His expression told her that he thought she had gone mad.

She stood at the open kitchen door, one minute shivering uncontrollably, then hot with fever. Cooley was approaching on his horse, followed by six neighbors, walking. They all looked to her like strangers, and she herself was someone she did not know. He tied his horse to the hitching post, and the others began searching in the yard. He walked toward her, slowly, so slowly that he might not ever reach her.

"My husband is not home," she said in a voice that was not hers. She watched him retrace his steps, then pause near the gate and kick an unnatural-looking heap of snow. He recovered what was underneath and came back. "I think that this is Mr Spooner's hat," he said. "And his meerschaum pipe?"

"It is his hat." Slowly, slowly she reached out and took the pipe. Then, in an explosion of emotion, she hurled it across the yard. It smashed on the well curb, its shards splayed out across the ground.

She met Cooley's astonished gaze. "This all must seem incomprehensible to you," she said.

He threw up his hands, then turned and went toward Hinkley's place, apparently in search of clues. He had not walked thirty rods before the others called him back. "Over here!" they shouted from the well.

The well! The look of terror on Ross's face, Brooks struggling to take off his bloody clothes, Buchanan breaking open Joshua's money box.

She could hear Cooley ordering somebody to go for Dr King. He himself would get the coroner, he said. Then he was at the kitchen door again. "I'm terribly sorry, ma'am," he said. "Your husband, we found him in the well. Looks like foul play."

Everything inside her began working in reverse.

"Don't worry, ma'am." He reached out to steady her. "We'll find whoever did this. I've already sent out an alarm."

The doctor arrived. The men brought in the body and laid it on the floor of the east parlor. "Beaten until dead," she heard the doctor say. Breathing became torture, her chest was in a vice. She was shivering, freezing, but could not make it to the settle by the fire. She sat down at the kitchen table and held her throbbing head.

Cooley came back. "The doctor is examining the remains. He says that you should come." His voice was gentle.

Her eyes darkened as she stared at him. "That is not possible," she said.

"I'm sorry, ma'am. I know it is a dreadful thing to put you through, but someone in the family must identify the corpse."

For God's sake! Do it yourself! You and your men all knew Joshua, knew him well, the doctor, too. "It's quite impossible!" No argument could sway her.

The coroner approached and asked her where the children were. Thinking that he wanted to make certain they were shielded from this evil, she assured him they were safe at Mrs Stratten's. Only later was she told that forthwith he went to fetch them and returned with Baby Bath, the other two, understanding more, having protested fiercely. The three-year-old was led to the east parlor and asked if the man there was her father. Wide-eyed and serious, she stared at the mutilated corpse and inquired if all dead men looked like that.

Earlier that morning, well before the sun was up, the Regulars and Ross, sobered by their frost-filled midnight trek, were back at Mrs Walker's. With Prudence at her side, Mary Walker let them in. "What's going on at such an hour?" she asked. "You scoundrels said you'd be in Brookfield for awhile."

"We never got to Brookfield," Buchanan lied. "We had a little complication. Mrs Spooner intercepted us in Leicester, met Brooks and me at the Tavern there to warn us that the Springfield guard had been called out to track us down. Some trumped-up charge about blowing up the magazine. That being the circumstance, we thought we'd better come back here."

Pru looked dubious and nodded toward Ross. "Where'd you pick him up?"

"Mrs Spooner turned him over to our care. She said she'd found him wandering about, claiming he was lost, and you know us, always happy to do a fellow a good turn."

"So you know Mrs Spooner?" Pru asked Ross.

"I don't know as I do, I just met her on the road. I know Mr Spooner, though, went on a trip with him to Lancaster awhile back."

Pru burst out laughing. "Sounds mighty queer to me." She wagged her finger at Brooks. "Been shopping? Them clothes ain't what you left in."

Mary led the Regulars to the room they'd occupied before. "There's space up in the loft," she said to Ross.

Later, about noon, Buchanan woke up sick. Brooks wasn't anywhere about. "Fetch me hot water and a bleeding bowl," he called to Mary Walker when he heard her clattering down the hall.

"You don't look too good," she said as she put down a crock of steaming water. He lowered his hand in it and as soon as his veins were swollen, he made a fist, and ordered her to tie a rag above his wrist. He pumped his hand, then asked her to undo the rag. Grimacing, he slid into the chosen vein the lancet he had taken from his pocket. "Hold the bowl up proper!" he roared. Mary sucked in her breath and looked the other way as his blood arched into it. When the operation was complete, Buchanan stanched the wound, and sent her off. He waited for a dizzy spell to pass, then, cursing his nervousness, went down to look for Brooks.

No one was in the taproom except Mary. "That Ezra fellow's up there looking strange," she said as she filled his glass. "Walks up and down and knocks his head against the wall, shaking like the Devil's in his guts. I asked him what was making him so weird."

"Yeah? How did he account for it?"

"'Reason enough,' he told me."

Buchanan swirled his rum around, muttering that Ross could be a problem if he came down with a case of conscience. He looked up to see Brooks reeling through the door, announcing in a boozy voice that he had stopped by Brown's Tavern, where the patrons had shown an uncommon interest in his watch and silver buckles.

"You stupid fuck!"

Buchanan was still haranguing when Pru burst in, her black face shining. "Murder in Brookfield!" she announced. "Someone I bet you fellows know, Mrs Spooner's husband, beat to death last night. The Committee's meeting now, over at Brown's Tavern." She stared at the initials on the silver buckles on Brooks' shoes. "Uh-huh," she said. "J S."

Brooks leered at Pru, and showed her Joshua's watch. Hands on her hips, she laughed at him. "Now where'd you come by anything so fancy? Did you inherit it from someone who is dead?"

Brooks was too far gone to notice the approach of the Committee. Not until they were on top of him did he realize that he was trapped. He looked to Buchanan, who raised both hands, palms out, and shook his head.

Whitney, a Committeeman, glanced around the room. "Where's the other one?" he asked. "The folks in Brookfield told us there were three." Leaving two of his men in charge of the two Regulars, he went in search of Ross, and found him cringing in the upper loft. "I need a minister," Ezra begged. "I'm guilty, but I didn't strike the fatal blow."

"You can tell us all about it soon enough," Whitney replied. He helped Ross down the ladder and tied his hands behind his back.

Within minutes, all three men were locked up in the Worcester county gaol.

Meanwhile, fourteen citizens of Brookfield, jurors for the inquest into Joshua Spooner's death, found that the deceased, "on the evening of the first of March, about nine of the clock, returning home from his neighbors, near his own door was feloniously assaulted by one or more persons unknown, knocked down, beat and bruised, and thrown into his own well with water in it, by persons to the jury unknown."

At noon news arrived from Worcester. Buchanan, Brooks, and Ross had admitted to the crime, and during his examination by the Justice of the Peace, Buchanan had implicated Mrs Spooner, as well as Mrs Stratten, Jesse Parker, and Alexander Cummings. On hearing this, the jurors ordered Mrs Spooner to take the test for culpability. She had no choice but to follow them and Dr King to the closed pine coffin in Joshua's east parlor. "It won't be pleasant, ma'am," the doctor said. "But you need only touch him for a moment."

She wanted to shout back at him. She knew the rule, everybody did. Men had been convicted on the strength of it. If Joshua's flesh appeared to glow when she placed her hand upon his forehead, she would be counted guilty.

The coroner lifted the coffin lid, and the stink of rotting flesh escaped. A bitter taste rose in Bathsheba's throat as, with half-closed eyes, she laid a finger near Joshua's matted hairline. The jury, watching breathlessly, saw the glow that they were looking for, just as she had known they would.

When the foreman said that she must go to gaol, the enormity of the part she'd played crashed down on her. "If it were not for this," she whispered, "I could meet my Judge. This all happened because Ross was sick at our house. That started it." The foreman looked embarrassed in the presence of such anguish. "The guilt lies entirely with the Regulars and me. I cannot blame anyone. This thing is my own doing." She flared with anger when she heard that Mrs Stratten, Alex, and Jesse had also been arrested. "They are not guilty! They weren't even there. Mrs Stratten has been caring for my children. What will become of them if you take her to the gaol?"

"They are with your sister Martha now," the foreman replied quietly. "They'll be all right."

Bathsheba accepted Ephraim Cooley's help as she stepped into Obediah Rice's sleigh. She sat impassive between Alex and Mrs Stratten. "Jesse has been taken on ahead," Obediah told her.

A light snow began to fall, and for awhile no one spoke. Then, after a few miles, Bathsheba repeated that Jesse and Mrs Stratten should not have been arrested. Nor Alex. It was just like Buchanan, the coward, implicating them, no doubt figuring that if he spread the guilt around, it would dilute the penalty. "I would gladly suffer ten deaths for each of them before they should suffer anything. They're innocent," she insisted. "Leave them alone."

She sat rigid as stone, bent slightly forward, as though listening for something. Her dark hat framed her face against the sparkling snow. Her eyes were bright, as though she had a fever. "I had a great desire to see Papa. If I could have gone to him, this murder would not have been committed." Obediah shook his head. There was no understanding any of this.

It was evening by the time Rice drew up beside Brown's Tavern. "We'll have some supper before going to the gaol," he said. Bathsheba had not eaten for two days, and, still repelled by food, she motioned the servant girl away. Rice handed her some biscuits and a glass of sherry. As she sipped, she again insisted that the crime was all her fault. "The effect of bad company," she kept repeating.

As they approached the gaol, Bathsheba recalled her visit to see Nathan, a lifetime ago. By now, he must have heard some version of the murder. She'd been told that the news, altered and embellished with each telling, was making its way through the whole of Worcester County and far beyond. What must he be thinking? And the others whom she loved—her mother, her siblings, Uncle John? How much did the children know? Had the news spread as far as Long Island? No doubt they all were condemning her to hell.

Outside the gaol, in the wavering light of torches, a mob was yelling at the single guard standing at the door. "Get more security! The Regulars are dangerous!" The crowd cursed the authorities for neglecting to replace the sheriff who had died several months ago, leaving nobody in charge. The Committee should be sued for negligence, for not replacing him immediately. Anything might happen in this crisis. "Arrest everyone who looks suspicious," someone yelled, and everyone took up the chant.

When Bathsheba came in view, the mob shifted its hostility to her. Men, as well as women, even children, shouted epithets—so many words for "whore."

Alex was taken to the dungeon to join Jesse, the Regulars, and Ross. The gaoler, Ephriam Curtis, showed Mrs Stratten to a corner cell. "I remember you," Mrs Curtis said as she locked Bathsheba in a cubicle directly opposite the central fire. "You came here a year or so ago to visit that traitor. Wasn't his name Danforth?"

"How long will I have to wait?" Bathsheba asked when Curtis came to check that she was properly secured.

He told her the Superior Court of Judicature would not meet for the grand jury hearing until April twenty-first. Almost seven weeks from now, she thought, enough time to grow old. She felt nauseous and faint. "Please leave me now," she said.

She sat down on her cot and watched the shadows from the gaoler's lantern dissolve in darkness. Close as the fire was, it was not close enough. Cold and damp spread over her. She wrapped the rough blanket from the cot around her shoulders and laid her hands across her belly, staring into the night at the black, uncertain path that lay ahead.

Chapter 27

"You'd best get dressed as soon as possible," Mrs Curtis said when she brought Bathsheba's toast and coffee. "My husband will be letting townsfolk in at eight."

It was appalling. Strangers would be paying for a glimpse of her, the woman who, everyone was saying, had arranged to have her husband murdered in order to be free to marry Ezra Ross, the youngster she had taken as her lover. The viewing fee, to be used to help defray the cost of guards, would include the privilege of going to the dungeon to ogle at the men. Treating us like freaks, Bathsheba thought. Unconscionable! Her mood had changed over the course of a sleepless night from contrition to smoldering fury, but she would control her anger, rise above the insults she was being forced to suffer. She would prove that she was still a Ruggles.

She dressed carefully and arranged her hair in a French twist. She chose from her trunk strands of colored floss and a pillowcase she had started to embroider months ago. Despite her desperate plight and the wretchedness of her surroundings, she was would spend the morning creating a bouquet of roses.

Viewers, mostly women, some with children tugging at their skirts, began to file past the cell, staring, sneering, dropping scurrilous remarks. "She don't look much like a whore," they told each other. Instead, she looked detached, beautiful and proud, too proud. Her bearing, aristocratic and erect, did not match her situation. There she was, quietly embroidering, never glancing up or giving any sign. Perhaps she was a witch. "Ye should be tarred and feathered here and now," one old woman taunted. "And rode on a rail till your whoring ass is slit up to your belly."

Bathsheba continued with her stitching.

At noon, gaoler Curtis closed the doors to paying visitors, but others soon replaced them. The Reverend Ebenezer Parkman came all the way from Westborough to lecture Mrs Spooner about her deviation from the paths of righteousness, then hurried home to write a fiery sermon, damning her to hell. Sister Martha came to say she had arranged for Joshua's interment in the Tufts' new family plot. She promised to take care of the children until everything was settled. "Don't bring them here," Bathsheba said. "I don't want them to remember me like this." Mary's husband, Dr Green, arrived with wine and cake and professional concern. "Your sister sends her love, and regrets she cannot visit you. She's ill." He did not add that it was the shock of hearing of the crime that had brought Mary to her bed.

The following afternoon, Mrs Curtis showed Sheba to the cell. How staunch she is, Bathsheba thought, in her seventy-fifth year riding some thirty miles from Hardwick through mud and slush against the raw March winds. They embraced with tears.

Sheba gestured toward the bag of books she'd brought, and the hamper full of breads and jams. "Your Uncle John's idea," she said. "He will come to see you when he can. He's been staying with me the past few weeks, ill again with the catarrh that plagues him every spring. Not so ill, though, that he's insensitive to what you're going through. He lies abed repeating that whatever you have done, he's sure there was a reason." Sheba paused. "Can you talk about it? Can you tell?"

Avoiding her mother's gaze, Bathsheba rose and peered through the bars of her tiny window. "There were many reasons, one of them unspeakable." She turned then, and faced her mother. "To the point of madness, I wanted Joshua dead. Not the way it happened, though." Her eyes expressed her pain as she admitted she had kept bad company. "I let the Devil lure me, and I lost my self."

Sheba reached out and touched her daughter's cheek. "It was that bad?"

"Yes." For several minutes, neither woman spoke. Then, "I want you to know that what they're saying about me and Ross is false. He's just a boy who was nice to me when I was in need. He was in love with me in his adolescent way, and I was good to him."

Sheba nodded.

"I've been sick with apprehension that you'd all despise me for bringing down the Ruggles name."

Sheba shook her head. "Never. Nathan, just recently returned from Maine, came by to see me yesterday. He assured me we could count on his support. He wanted me to tell you that he'll visit you before the week is out."

' "Tell him to come soon. Please."

"I understand."

They talked about the Brigadier, agreeing that it would be foolhardy to try to contact him and ask for help. "Not that he wouldn't risk his life for you," Sheba said. "There was a time when his extensive knowledge of the law would have made a difference, but that's no longer so." Now the legal system was unreliable at best, the judges inexperienced, most of the good ones, like the Brigadier, in exile. He could not be of help, even if some miracle allowed him to return to Massachusetts. He would only be a hindrance, his hated presence fanning the people's animosity against his daughter.

"Do you think he knows what's happened?" Bathsheba asked.

"The news has reached Long Island, I've been told. His friends are trying to shield him from it."

Bathsheba sniffed dismissal of such attempts. "Not likely," she said.

Again the two women sat in silence. Then, "Mama," Bathsheba whispered. "Mama, will they hang me?"

Bathsheba had another visitor who stopped by every day. Tall and thin, with black, penetrating eyes, the Reverend Thaddeus Maccarty was old enough to be her father, but shared little else in common with the Brigadier. As a youth, he'd gone to sea, but his health had failed, forcing him to quieter pursuits. After preparing for the ministry at Harvard College, he was called to Kingston, south of Boston, but his compassionate approach to sinners was at odds with the elders' views about damnation, and he was asked to leave. It wasn't long, however, before he was installed at Old South Church in Worcester, where he'd been the pastor for three decades now.

Bathsheba received him graciously, but with her usual candor. "Barring my grandfather, a much loved clergyman, my family is not known for reverence, and I've never felt the need for ministers." She looked up from her embroidery. "I can't think of turning to you now just because my situation is precarious. Someone in your parish is no doubt waiting for you as we speak. Don't waste your time on me."

"I hope that in the end my visits will not prove to be a waste of time." His voice was quiet, comforting. "But I'll intrude no more today. Tomorrow for a little while, perhaps."

Over the long weeks of a wet March, stretching into chilly April, there was one caller who made the prison walls dissolve. His visits were always casual, an old and trusted friend just dropping by. "I have an opportunity to buy a fine bull calf," Nathan told her the first time he came. "I've just followed up on a lead at the Harnden Farm right here in Worcester. This morning I arranged with the owner to take the animal awhile, try him out, as you might say. I've brought him with me, and he's just outside. Come over to the window. I'd value your opinion."

Bathsheba stood by Nathan's side while they discussed the calf tethered in the gaol yard—his pedigree, his legs, his head, features that might make the beast a winner. "He reminds me of Papa's prize bull, Lord Paramount, when he was little," she said.

Together they recalled the bullfight fourteen years ago, Nathan's first bull against the invincible Lord Paramount. "Remember?" Bathsheba asked. It had been a bright, hot August morning. She was eighteen then, and in love with Nathan. She never had stopped loving him, not really.

"Remember?" she repeated. Another time, another world. "Nathan, you should buy that animal."

"It's settled then," he said. "I'll name him Paramount for you."

She slipped her hand in his, grateful for his presence. Her pleasure in his company was simple and intense. Death by execution, should it come to that, seemed less horrifying when she was with him.

Chapter 28

It was the Reverend Maccarty who brought Bathsheba the results of the Grand Jury hearing, held, at last, as scheduled, on Tuesday, April twenty-first, Seventeen Hundred Seventy Eight. "They found for a True Bill," he told her as he placed a bouquet of violets from his garden on the stone sill of her cell window. "There's more than enough evidence to justify a trial." Neither of them was surprised.

Levi Lincoln, chosen by the Massachusetts Revolutionary Council to represent Bathsheba and the soldiers, seemed to her discouragingly young for such a job, but he was earnest. "The new Attorney General, recently appointed by the Council, will be the prosecuting lawyer," he informed her. "Robert Treat Paine. Perhaps you've heard of him."

She had, of course. She had followed his prosecution of the soldiers after the Boston massacre. "Moreover, during the French and Indian War, Mr Paine was a chaplain, briefly, for my father's troops. I remember Papa mentioning that he wrote flowery verses." It would be folly to say more.

"I fear he won't be flowery at the trial," Mr Lincoln warned. He handed her a copy of the True Bill of Indictment. Brooks was charged with murder by "striking, beating, kicking the said Joshua Spooner in the back, head, stomach, sides and throat, thereby inflicting several mortal wounds of which the victim died." Ross and Buchanan, the Indictment charged, had, with malice and aforethought, aided, abetted, comforted, and maintained Brooks.

Bathsheba drew in her breath and gazed at Lincoln blankly before going on to the part about herself. "Bathsheba Spooner," it said, "not having God before her eyes, but being seduced by the instigation of the Devil, before the felony and murder aforesaid, on the twenty-eighth day of February last, willfully, and of her malice aforethought did incite, move, abet, counsel and procure, against the peace of the Government and people." The words blurred over as she read.

"It's right about the Devil," she said, her voice strained from trying to hide her anguish. She thought a moment and then read again. "This says nothing about Mrs Stratten, Jesse, and Alex."

"They're going to turn state's evidence," Lincoln said, dismissing them. "Let's get back to you. Let's suppose you did exactly as the Indictment says, but then at the last minute you relented." If he could prove that, maybe he could get her off, provided the raging sentiments against her could be tamed. He explained that, in the eyes of the law, one is not counted an accessory before the fact if one is not pressing for the crime at the time it is committed.

"I did not press, nor did I raise a hand against it." It was painful to admit this to a stranger and she did it only because her father had often emphasized that complete disclosure by a client was essential for a trial lawyer to succeed. She never would tell this man everything, she couldn't, but she so wanted Mr Lincoln to understand at least a little. "I wanted Mr Spooner out of all our lives. So did the others. There were reasons." But Lincoln showed no interest in motives. "The deed itself was dreadful," she added.

Lincoln stood up to leave. "You'll be arraigned on Thursday. Plead not guilty and put yourself for trial."

Even before dawn on Friday, the crowd outside the Worcester County Court House was much too large to be contained within. Sensing the potential for a riot if too many citizens were turned away, William Greenleaf, the newly appointed sheriff, changed the venue of the trial to the much larger Old South Meeting House. He made it known that he did so with reluctance, and urged against anybody misinterpreting the move. Sentiment about the case was fiercely charged with politics, involving as it did a blatant Tory and two English Regulars, and Greenleaf knew that the Meeting House was far from neutral ground in many minds. From its balcony the Declaration of Independence had been read for the first time in New England, making Old South emblematic of the rebel cause. "But let no one," he declared, "conclude that I have any hidden motives here."

Farmers and their families soon filled the sixty-one box pews, and by eight o'clock, even the aisles and the steps leading to the galleries were jammed. Latecomers, denied admittance, gathered outside near open windows to catch scraps of the proceedings or a glimpse of the defendants, especially Mrs Spooner.

Not a whisper could be heard, not a cry from the young children scattered through the crowd, as Bathsheba and the soldiers were led from the vestry, past the jurors, to the makeshift dock beside the pulpit. The bailiff announced in loud and somber tones that the law required that all four defendants stand throughout the whole of the proceedings. Bathsheba breathed consciously and deeply, fearful that she might fail to endure. She must not squander energy on unnecessary motion or emotion. She froze herself in place.

Five judges emerged and took their places at a table. Even without the red silk robes and powdered wigs worn by their predecessors who had served the Crown, the men looked massive and formidable. Chief Justice Cushing was forty-six years old with twenty-seven years before the bar. Of his four Associates—Jedediah Foster, Nathaniel Peaslee Sergeant, David Sewall, and James Sullivan—Foster was the only man Bathsheba knew. He'd been Brookfield's representative in the General Court for years, and in the early days he'd been an ally of her father. Later he was swept into the rebel camp, and after all the Loyalist judges were ousted, the new regime, hard put to find qualified replacements, appointed Foster, despite his minimal experience at law.

Stone-faced, Bathsheba scanned the crowd. Everyone seemed hostile, and she longed for a sympathetic presence—her mother, perhaps, or Uncle John, or Nathan. But Sheba had told them all to stay away. "Everybody knows that we are Loyalists," she said. "And our presence would only make bad matters worse."

Judge Cushing called the court to order. "I must remind the prisoners that during the proceedings, they will not be allowed to speak, not under any circumstance."

It makes no difference, Bathsheba thought. Nothing she could say would help. No one would believe her in the first place, and if she tried to establish that she had serious, justifiable disagreements with her husband, she would be charged with yet another crime; a woman's criticism of her spouse was not allowed in Massachusetts.

Prosecutor Paine appeared with a flourish. Bathsheba thought he looked ridiculous, and, if it had been the old days and she met him at a party, she would have laughed at him. What she had heard was true: since his appointment as Attorney General he had taken to dressing in true macaroni style, elegantly attired, his hair arranged in a prodigious foretop, with ear curls and a queue. Papa had been right about the man.

After presenting the Indictment, Paine asked the bailiff to bring in Dr King.

The doctor testified that the victim had been savagely attacked. With professional detachment, he described Mr Spooner's cheeks and temple, black with bruises, the sockets of his eyes sunk deep into his skull, his broken bones, his waxy skin. A gash across the victim's scalp cut to the bone.

It all came back, Brooks lunging with his massive hulk to smash out Joshua's brains, his ponderous boot-clad foot crashing down on Joshua's ribs, the sickening sound of cracking bones. Then, in excruciating contrast, there arose the vision of a handsome, youthful Joshua standing before her in the moonlight in Nathan's garden, seducing her.

Mary Walker was now telling what she thought she remembered about Bathsheba's visits to the tavern. Although her testimony did not bear directly on the crime, and was often contradictory, she nonetheless succeeded in reinforcing the strongly held opinion that Bathsheba was a whore. "She came and went," Mary said. "She was often with the Sergeant, and she brought him a length of lovely cloth, quite fancy." Wistfully she touched her skirt, made of rough homespun. "Payment for the job she wanted him to do, I'll wager, smuggled in from England by her Tory friends."

Paine told her to stick to facts and keep opinions to herself, but the damage was already done, and there was more. "Private William Brooks once laid his head down on her shoulder, and when I gave her a look, she said, 'You must not wonder. Billy has lived at my house and is as fond of me as he would be of a mother.'"

A hum of "I-told-you-so" went through the crowd.

Liar! She would have preferred to die rather than let Brooks come near her. But no one was going to question Mary's word; she was saying what everyone was there to hear. And she was still going on. "Later, Mrs Spooner was in the Sergeant's room, and they were talking—about poison, I think it must have been, him wrapping up some powders, making out that it was calomel for Mrs Spooner to take to a sick child. I could tell that they were lying."

On and on, the crowd responding with swells of "ohs" and "ahs," and Mary looking pleased with her performance.

Bathsheba shot her an accusing glance. The girl lowered her eyes, and, turning to the judges, asked, "Can I go now? I'm very tired, sirs."

"Continue with your questioning." Judge Cushing gave Mr Paine the nod.

The prosecutor smoothed one of his ear curls. "What happened when Mrs. Spooner left your mother's tavern on Saturday, February twenty-eighth?"

Mary bit her nails, looking first at Bathsheba, then Buchanan. She ran her tongue around her lips, and smiled as if gratified that Mr Paine was so interested in what she had to say. "Well, before Mrs Spooner left, she told the sergeant, 'Remember, tomorrow night at eleven o'clock.' He replied the same."

Bathsheba studied the jury, and what she saw convinced her they already had made up their minds. Understandably. Everyone had heard how bad she was, breaking all the Ten Commandments all at once. Everybody talked about it all the time. And everything that Mary said corroborated this opinion.

Prudence backed up Mary's story about the powders. She had gone up for her broom in the closet by Buchanan's room and had seen for herself bits of what was going on, although, she admitted, she had trouble hearing what was being said.

After a string of witnesses told when they'd seen the Regulars and Ross at one time or another at the Spooner house, Judge Cushing called for an adjournment of an hour.

It had begun to rain, and Bathsheba shivered as she walked beside her guard past Mower's Tavern, Isaiah Thomas' printing office, and the Court House. Mrs Curtis was waiting at the gaol with a bowl of mutton stew, but Bathsheba shook her head. The smell of the over-boiled meat brought on a wave of nausea, and she lay down on her cot, trying to suppress the suspicion that had begun to plague her. Surely she was suffering from nothing more than simple nervousness. God, let it be just nervousness.

When the court resumed, Alex Cummings told how he brought in the Regulars the day the blizzard started.

"Did you ever hear conversations between Mrs Spooner and the Sergeant?"

"Oh, yes. When they were in the sitting room and I was in the kitchen, even with the door between full shut, I could hear them if I tried."

"And?"

"A day or two after the Regulars arrived, I heard Mrs Spooner tell the Sergeant she could no longer live with Mr Spooner."

Murmurs rose. Bathsheba clenched her hands. Yes, she had said that. She had confided in a stranger whom she thought she'd never see again. Fool!

Now Alex was saying that Mr Spooner did not like the look of Brooks. "He desired his wife to get the soldiers off, or else he'd send for the Committee."

"The Committee on Safety?" Paine asked.

"Yes, sir."

And on and on.

No, Alex testified, he had not been a witness to the murder, he had been out in the barn with Mrs Stratten. "But later, when I went back to the house, I smelled burning wool. Brooks' breeches were sizzling on the fire in the sitting room, and the three soldiers were shifting into different clothes. Mrs Spooner was having a hard time trying to open Mr Spooner's money box, the one he always kept in the mahogany chest. She gave it to the Sergeant, and he smashed it with the poker. She divided up the money, back and forth between the soldiers."

"Did she give anyone anything else?"

"She took Mr Spooner's silver buckles from the Sergeant. I guess he'd swiped them off his shoes before they dumped him in the well. She bade me go get some water to wash off the blood. She said I could have them, but I said no. I got Mrs Stratten to go out with me, but we couldn't dip the bucket. Mrs Spooner asked why we didn't get the water. I said I thought Mr Spooner was down there at the bottom. She said it was not true. Mrs Stratten was much frighted and she cried and run and got the Bible. I asked Mrs Spooner if they'd cut Mr Spooner's throat. She said, 'No, they knocked him down.'"

Paine asked Alex if he had anything to add, and Alex looked straight at Bathsheba, waited a long moment, and then said, "About a month before the murder, Mrs Spooner asked me to do the job, saying if I did, she would make a man of me."

Spectators gasped. Bathsheba glared at Alex. They had never liked each other, and now he had the upper hand. Why wasn't Lincoln cross-examining him to bring out how he'd conspired side by side with the three others? Bathsheba reined in her racing thoughts. Could it be that Lincoln didn't know? There had been only two days between the indictment and the trial, and Lincoln had seen her only once, with few questions even then. Her father would never have allowed this nightmare to go on like this.

Jesse and Mrs Stratten took the stand but added nothing. True, Lincoln did not pick up on Buchanan's allegations, he did not ask Mrs Stratten why she stood by silently while murder plans went forward, nor did he cross examine Jesse about his plotting with the soldiers. But couldn't one or both of them say something, a few words, some indication that she was not a murderer at heart? Couldn't they try to rescue her reputation, cast doubt on her perceived unmitigated wickedness? They both knew her well, they had been friends. Even if Paine's line of questioning left little chance for wandering off course, couldn't they somehow have worked in something? Instead, they betrayed her.

Two of the remaining witnesses, did, however, dare to say a mitigating word or two. Mary Parks, a neighbor, testified that she had never heard Mrs Spooner wish her husband dead or intimate in any way that she wanted to get rid of him. "She merely said sometimes that she did not love her home." Which, of course, was crime enough.

Sally Bragg, a friend of Jesse's, testified that he had told her more than once about how bad a man Mr Spooner was. Bad to his wife, bad just for his drink, bad for things Jesse could not bring himself to mention. But all this was only hearsay.

The hour was late, and, although Paine was noted for his long winded summations, he let this case rest without too many words, apparently convinced he had already won.

Lincoln, however, did not let the jurors off so easily. Diligent and inexperienced, he had much to say. Earnest in his plea for justice, he began by referring to the unusual importance of the case. Not only was it the first capital offense to be tried by the new government, it also involved an unprecedented number of defendants. He begged the jurors to rise above the rampant prejudice and public sentiment, and urged that they ignore all hearsay and irrelevant political considerations.

He made no attempt to argue for the Regulars, and turned immediately to Ross. Although he might be guilty of misconduct and tried for such, there was no evidence to prove that he ever truly meant to kill. His confession could not be used against him. "Confessions are often given out of fear or misdirected hopes for mercy," Lincoln pointed out. "Take into account that if Mr Ross had a design against

Mr Spooner's life, he had frequent opportunities to take it—at his house, at Princeton, and on the road. The murder had long been contemplated, and Ross's failure to carry through shows that he had no real intent to do it, but only wished to keep up the appearance of intention, perhaps to impress Mrs Spooner."

Lincoln was about to launch his defense of her, and she strained to catch his every word. She was certain he would make the case that she'd had second thoughts at the last minute, and therefore was not culpable. Maybe, just maybe, there was a chance.

But he was not going down that road. "It has been rumored," he began, "that Mrs Spooner was on ill terms with her husband. This is to trump up one crime that there may seem to have been a motive for another." The next minute he was talking about her judgment. "With her fine background and appearance, she might have had any gallant she pleased, not such a one as Ross."

Not such a one as Ross! Bathsheba raged silently against the lawyer. Misleading, pejorative, putting down a youth who almost lost his life serving the cause of men like you! And you, daring to assume what everybody else assumes, what nobody can prove, and what is false, that we were lovers.

Lincoln was now raising the question of her sanity. "Would she have taken this youth of low position, unfitting to her rank and station, if she had been of a sane mind?"

Of sane mind! The jury might well swallow his unquestioning acceptance of the gossip, his unjust characterization of Ezra, and his appalling logic, but nobody would buy this insanity idea. Even if he could convince the jury that she was raving mad, they wouldn't let her off. Just the opposite; society has no place for lunatics.

Then there shot through her mind an explanation for Lincoln's switch from the plea that might have got her off. Maybe, if he had gone ahead and argued that she'd changed her mind and therefore was not culpable, maybe, if he'd done that, his promising career would be cut short. To vindicate a Tory would hardly be acceptable.

"What end could the killing of her husband serve?" he was asking now. "Even if not apprehended, she would deprive her children of their father and guardian, herself of a husband, and would subject herself to the burdens of her family with only one third of his estate, the maximum the law allows for widows whose husbands have not directed otherwise. Can there be any doubt that Mrs Spooner was incapable of thinking straight? I submit that her state of mind at the time the murders were committed renders her not guilty."

Hopeless.

Heavy with exhaustion, Bathsheba heard Judge Cushing give the charge and declare adjournment until eight o'clock the following morning. "At which hour, I expect to hear the verdict." There was no time to waste, too many other cases on the docket.

Chapter 29

"Guilty. We find all four prisoners guilty."

Bathsheba had the impression that every member of the jury, every last farmer among them, had singled her out as the most guilty of them all. Not really hearing, she listened to Attorney General Paine move the Court for the only sentence allowed by law for murder. She was conscious of a hush falling over the assembly as Judge Cushing brought down his gavel. "The prisoners," he intoned, pronouncing each of their names with weighty emphasis, "are herewith sentenced to be severally hanged by the neck till dead on a date as yet to be determined by the Revolutionary Council." Then, before proceeding to the other cases scheduled for the session, he ordered that Sarah Stratten, Alexander Cummings, and Jesse Parker, all having served the state as witnesses, should be forthwith set free.

So that's why they had not said anything to help her! Until this moment, Bathsheba had not fully understood that their total cooperation with the prosecution was required if they were to avoid imprisonment or death.

The soldiers were led out, shackled at their wrists, iron chains linking them together. Ross was crying. He should not have been condemned, he was so young, he hadn't really done a thing, except steal Joshua's horse. Her heart went out to him. She nodded to Buchanan, who looked distressed, for once. Brooks wasn't worth a glance. She gazed straight ahead as she held out her hands to be bound with a loose cord.

Stately and erect, she walked between her guards, ignoring taunts, infuriating those who'd come to see her humbled. In truth, she was almost unaware of the tumult going on around her, only that within. Sentenced to an obscene public death, she had just been told her life

161

was almost over. A man with the authority to do so had announced it to the world. On this balmy April morning, the first warm day in many months, full of promise, she, Bathsheba Ruggles Spooner, had just been told that the government of her country was going to hang her by the neck at some prescribed hour in the middle of her life, the time to be determined not by God or nature, but by men.

The distance from the Old South Meeting House to the gaol was short, but the walk seemed endless, like walking through a nightmare. It struck her as unbearable that the clumps of wild primroses along the road, which had been so fresh and lovely earlier, were now crushed and trampled by the crowd. A squirrel scampered across the road, and a boy about the age of Little Josh ran after it, then stopped and looked at her, smiling inexplicably. She imagined that she saw her children there beside him—Little Josh, Elizabeth, Baby Bath—confused and vulnerable.

As the prisoners and their guards approached the gaol, Bathsheba recognized the frail-looking man standing near the door, a sheaf of papers in one hand, a wicker basket in the other. His curls stuck out in all directions from underneath his hat. Although the day was mild, he wore a heavy coat, and perspiration glistened on his forehead. Forgetting that her hands were tied, she tried to wave a greeting. Hampered by the cord, her efforts appeared comic, and derisive snickers spread throughout the crowd.

"Shua!" Uncle John called out. "Wait a minute. Listen."

She indicated to her guards that she had a great desire to hear what he was saying, and they paused.

"That Curtis woman who does for you won't let me in. I begged. I told her who I was. She looked at me like I was crazy. She was rude. She shooed me off."

One of the guards touched Bathsheba's elbow to urge her on. "Don't go away," she called back as she was ushered across the threshold of the gaol.

Mrs Curtis was waiting in the dim interior. "I've heard, ma'am, and I am sorry," she said. "I'm not wise enough to make out why I think it, but they should have let you off. Here, let me free your hands."

Bathsheba pled with Mrs Curtis. "The gentleman outside, my uncle, Mr Ruggles. Help me through this evil day and allow him to be with me for a while. Mrs Curtis, please."

"Oh, ma'am, I do appreciate your circumstances, but this relative of yours, my husband told me not to let him in. He's not quite right, I think. He says he's come to visit for a week. When he arrived an hour or so ago and discovered you weren't here, he looked around, then went away, and came back with this." She pointed to a bucket and a bag of lime. "He said that while he's here he's going to whitewash everything. We can't have that, you know."

"Mrs Curtis, please bring my uncle to me."

"I can't do that. It's not only that he acts so strange, but Mr Curtis ordered that no one be admitted save for pastors and guards and folks like that. It's for your own good, ma'am. There's them out there who'd leave as not get rid of you right now and save the price of hanging."

"Go speak to him, at least." Bathsheba's face was white with urgency. "Make some excuse. He's sensitive. He mustn't think he's been shut out because you think he's daft."

A few minutes later Mrs Curtis came back with the sheaf of papers and the wicker basket. Beneath a white linen napkin were a dozen scones, and when Bathsheba loosened the ribbon from the papers, she found careful sketches of geometric shapes, lenses, prisms, all with problems written underneath in her uncle's miniscule eccentric hand. "Puzzles, queries, things to fill your mind," he had added in a note. "You'll make wonderful discoveries, find truths, real truths."

How dear of him. It was painful beyond endurance to be cut off forever from somebody she loved. Even the view from her tiny window distressed her, reminding her that never again could she walk through greening fields, white with early daisies. Oh, let the Council set an early date, let this all be over soon. No, not too soon, not until… She wished fervently that she believed in prayer.

As she imagined how the end would come, it occurred to her that sometime between the present and the moment of her death she might do something shameful, indecent, or unseemly. She had heard that people waiting for the noose sometimes went raving mad or became unable to restrain the functions their bodies normally controlled. That must not happen, not to her. She must walk with measured step to the most ignominious of deaths, with a dignity worthy of Uncle John, her parents and her siblings, worthy of centuries of Ruggleses, going back to royalty in France. Worthy of Nathan's love.

That evening, as the Reverend Maccarty walked from the rectory to the gaol, he prayed silently, asking God to give him wisdom and compassion. Until this morning, there had always been the possibility that Ezra Ross and Mrs Spooner might escape the gallows, but now the fate of all four prisoners seemed certain. Although the date of execution had not yet been set, he knew that he would not have long to try to help them save their souls. He was awed and humbled by the task before him.

He nodded a greeting to the guard and went below, pausing a moment to let his eyes adjust to the brown light in the dungeon.

The prisoners were sitting on their mats of straw, eating their meal of gruel. Each seemed lost and separate from the others, grizzled by fear and lack of sleep. They stood up deferentially, but Maccarty motioned them to be at ease. "It's almost over," he said quietly. "You'll soon be making retribution with your lives. Be thankful you can do so."

Buchanan scrambled to his feet, his swagger gone. "We were all crazy, Reverend. It was the drink, the Devil and the drink. God would not be unjust if He cast us off this very instant and made us burn in hell for all eternity."

Ross flinched.

Maccarty said a prayer and then suggested that they read a psalm together; he chose the fifty-first:

Have mercy upon me, O God, according to thy loving kindness: according unto the multitude of thy tender mercies blot out my transgressions.
Wash me thoroughly from mine iniquity, and cleanse me from my sin.
For I acknowledge my transgressions and my sin is ever before me.

The Reverend turned to Ross. "God blessed you with a good tenor voice," he said. "Please lead us in a hymn." Making the choice was simple: Brooks knew no hymn at all, and the only one Buchanan could remember was the beginning of "Our God Our Help in Ages Past," taught him by his mother when he was a little boy.

When they finished, the Reverend spoke with each man separately, then climbed the slippery stone steps. It was almost pleasant in Bathsheba's cell compared with the quarters he'd just left. She was working by candlelight on a puzzle Uncle John had brought. "You spent a long time with the men," she said. "I was afraid you might not come." Her words slipped out before she caught them. She hadn't really meant to put it that way, as if she had become dependent on his solace. She reached for her uncle's basket and offered him a scone. "A present from my Uncle John."

"Did the jury's verdict shock you?" Maccarty asked.

"No. It was inevitable after what they'd heard. I don't blame the jurors or the judges or Attorney General Paine. They were doing what they had to do. But Mr Lincoln and some of the witnesses did wrong by me."

The Reverend raised his eyebrows, questioning.

"My husband's death should be counted as a blessing," she finally said.

"I'm distressed to hear you speak that way." But he refrained from further comment.

"If you knew the circumstances, maybe you would understand," she added.

165

"Perhaps you should try to tell me. I don't think you realize how much I want you to confess and bow down with true contrition so that you may receive forgiveness through our Saviour and find peace."

Bathsheba looked deep into his eyes. "I'd like that too," she said. "I yearn for that, but true contrition is not an automatic thing. I hate the act of murder and the part I played in Joshua's death, but—and I know this will be incomprehensible to you—I feel no remorse." She waited for some response, but the Reverend gave none. "If I ever come to it," she added, "I'll make my confession only to my Maker, not to any man. Thank you, though, for your concern. I can see you truly care."

Maccarty rose and took her hand. "I'll be back tomorrow," he said.

Yes, he would come faithfully, and he would pray for her.

A week passed with seven visits from the Reverend. Sometimes Bathsheba sat with him a quarter of an hour or more without a word. When she spoke, she avoided talking of herself or of the murder, and would ask instead about the progress of the war or the latest shifts in politics. For his part, as frequently as he deemed wise, the Reverend tried to probe her heart.

How kind he is, Bathsheba thought, respectful, too. Eventually she started telling him about her children. "Their childhood has been so different from mine," she said. "Their home so full of shadows."

She picked up her embroidery.

"Were you forced to marry Mr Spooner?"

She shook her head. "I was very young and he was like no other man I'd ever known, charming, absolutely. My discovery of the real Mr Spooner after we were married confused me at first, then angered, then frightened me, and ultimately…"

"Your parents, if they did not force the marriage, did they approve?"

"My father did, but then, he was pre-occupied with his collapsing world. He saw that war was coming, and his affairs were going badly.

He believed that marriage would mean some measure of security for me."

"And your mother?"

"She saw through Mr Spooner, but I would not listen."

"What did she see? Or, put another way, what did you find out?"

"Life with him would always be a life in hell." She looked away. "Over the years I came to despise him with a hatred that destroyed me."

"I want to try to understand. Can you explain a little more?"

"No, Reverend, I cannot." She could never divulge the sordid depths, the corruption of her marriage. "It's doubtful," she continued, "that anyone as good as you could ever understand that one can be forced into depravity. When that happens, even the most debased and horrible thoughts come to seem quite ordinary, if repeated often enough. I fell into this trap, but you must believe me when I say that Mr Spooner's guilt was just as great as mine, or greater, really." She paused, expecting an argument, but the Reverend remained silent.

"I believe my trial was unjust," she went on. "There were so many things that should have been brought out. Moreover, in the old days, had my father handled such a case, I'm sure he would have insisted that each of us four defendants be tried separately. There was no justice here. But then, Reverend, what is justice? No matter. I've come to understand that my sentence is the price I have to pay. There can't be any other way, but I have no regrets and I make no progress toward contrition."

She slipped the embroidery hoops from the linen square on which she had been working, and smoothed the finished piece. In one corner of the handkerchief were the Reverend's initials, elegantly wrought with strands of light blue silk.

"To thank you for your kindness." She smiled as she handed it to him. "And to let you know I'm trying."

Several days later, Maccarty wrote in his journal:

Mrs Spooner is a person of uncommon fortitude of mind.
She does not for the most part appear to be affected by the

many circumstances in her case which deeply affect others. But she told me that she feels much more than she ever could express. It is clear that she is deeply troubled. Seldom a day passes but that I visit her, for which she expresses deepest gratitude. I try to converse with her on the main point, and to impress her with a sense of guilt, hoping to observe the symptoms of true penitence. But signs of this are quite discouraging. Since the trial, though, she has been more willing to discuss the conditions leading to her husband's death, saying that her life with him was not agreeable. Domestic dissentions went on from step to step until she conceived an utter aversion to him, for reasons she declines to talk about.
One thing is certain, though—her behavior toward me is always agreeable and polite. From the frequent opportunity I've had to be with her, I've come to know that she's a kind, obliging person of generous disposition.

In his next entry, May 9, 1778, the Reverend recorded that the Council had set the time of execution for Thursday, the fourth of June, between the hours of noon and four. "The men received this communication with great agitation," he wrote. "But Mrs Spooner seemed unmoved. I've learned, however, that, with her, appearances can deceive profoundly."

Chapter 30

During the next few weeks, the Reverend Maccarty not only counseled Bathsheba concerning the salvation of her soul, but he also tried to bring her some diversion from her thoughts about her fate and the tedium of her tiny cell. Because he'd learned that she found satisfaction and relief in following politics and the progress of the war, he shared with her one afternoon a letter he had just received. "It's from a friend in England," he explained. "He says that back in February we missed by very little making a settlement to end the war." He began to read aloud. "'Even as Mr Franklin was negotiating with the French, trying to get help for the American rebels, a Parliamentary commission in Britain was working out an offer of reconciliation with the colonies.'"

She knew she should be interested, but in her present state of mind she was having trouble even taking in the meaning of the words. When the Reverend paused and looked up, his face alive with eagerness for her reaction, she was unable to respond.

"Don't you see," he said, obviously disappointed. "Burgoyne's defeat at Saratoga was so crushing that the British reconsidered their position. Apparently the King was ready to give in, conceding everything short of independence. Parliament was prepared to repeal every Act objectionable to us. Think of it! If the British had moved just a little faster, or Dr Franklin a little slower, we might be at peace today."

I ought somehow to react, he's trying so hard to reach me. But I can't even feign an interest in either war or peace, not today. "There is something else that I must speak of," she said abruptly.

He waited, bending slightly forward, murmuring his thanks to God that at last she seemed ready to repent.

169

"I am carrying a child."

"Dear God!" Maccarty got up and stared out the window for what seemed like an eternity. When he finally spoke, Bathsheba hardly recognized his voice, so harsh, so unlike him. "How do you know?" Then slowly his expression changed from one of accusation to one of doubt and disappointment. "I mean, are you certain?"

"I know what you must be thinking." For centuries convicted women had falsely pled a pregnant state in order to obtain a stay of execution. "But in my case, that is not so. For weeks I have suspected my condition. There have been all the signs, and with each passing day, my concern has deepened. I kept hoping that it wasn't true, or at least that there would be no quickening before my life is ended. Then yesterday, I was certain it was happening, and at this very moment I can feel movement in my belly. I'm absolutely sure. And now it is too late to ask Mrs Curtis for extract of rue or oil of tansy to try to bring it off."

She returned Maccarty's troubled gaze. "It was lawfully conceived," she added, hoping that would make at least some difference, mitigate his censure.

But he did not look convinced.

"Yes," she repeated. "Conceived within the law, my husband's child." Joshua, sodden, wallowing in obscenity, Joshua the father. "Yes, Reverend, lawfully conceived."

Maccarty's penetrating eyes jolted her back to the gravity of her condition. "Can you instruct me what to do?" she asked. She knew there were men in Boston who had the power to save the child, but how could she get through to them? "How can I get the Revolutionary Council to believe me? It's clear that even you are skeptical."

The Reverend went back to the window and looked out, as if searching in the gaol yard for the answer. "Everyone will say the child belongs to Ross," he finally said.

"That has not escaped my thinking. But I cannot help what people say. Anyway, what difference does it make? The child is innocent."

Maccarty hesitated, his back still to her. The walls of the cell seemed to be closing in. This man in whom she had dared to place her

170

trust was going to abandon her. Of course. It was too much to expect a man of God to intervene in something as unholy as her plight.

"You are sure?" he asked again.

"I can't tell you how much your doubt distresses me."

He turned to face her. "I need some time on this," he said.

The next afternoon Maccarty handed her two closely written pages—a petition written in Buchanan's hand, and bearing his and Ross's signatures, separated by Brooks' mark. Beneath it was a paragraph the Reverend himself had written. "Please read all this carefully," he said. "Then, if you agree with the soldiers' statement, you can add your name to theirs. Tomorrow I'll take the document to Boston and personally deliver it."

Bathsheba went to the window for more light in order to decipher Buchanan's surprisingly elegant tiny penmanship, extravagantly embellished with flourishes and indentations:

> *To the honorable the Council for the state of Massachusetts Bay, in New England ~~~~~*
>
> *The humble petition of James Buchanan, William Brooks, Ezra Ross and Bathsheba Spooner ~~~~~*
>
> *Most Humbly Sheweth that your poor petitioners,, being Fearful of their unpreparedness to appear before their Maker and Judge after perpetrating so horrid a Crime, and they being informed by the Sherife the time of their execution would be the fourth day of June~~~~~~~~~~~*
>
> *Your poor petitioners do therefore most earnestly prey your Honors, that you would be pleased to grant them some longer time than the before mentioned, which, should your Honors in your great goodness grant them, they hope, and through the divine assistance*

and blessing upon the means used, trust they shall improve it to the valuable purposes, it being a matter which concerns their everlasting Salvation~~~~~~~~~~~~~~

They Most Humbly submit to your Honors' linety and Goodness,, and as in duty bound they will ever pray, etc, etc, etc~~~~~~~~~~~~~~~~

James Buchanan

his
William X Brooks
mark

Ezra Ross

Worcester Gaol
20ᵗʰ May 1778

A passage in Maccarty's handwriting was next:

Mr Maccarty's most dutiful respects wait upon the honorable board, begging leave humbly to represent to them, that he has had much opportunity to know the state of the above named prisoners; that he has found the men all along, and especially since their condemnation, to be much affected with their deplorable condition; freely acknowledging their heinous guilt, and the righteousness of the sentence pronounced against them. They appear to be very humble and penitent—to be much in earnest that they may make their peace with their Maker—much engaged in acts of devotion, and eager to embrace all opportunities, both public and private, for religious counsels and instruction. For which reasons Mr Maccarty presumes humbly to desire, that the prayer of their petition, as above, may be granted. And in that case he can assure your honors on his own behalf, and on the behalf of his brethren in the ministry, that all suitable endeavors will be used with them, in order, if it shall please God to succeed them, that they may be prepared for the solemn scene before them. And as to the unhappy woman, he would beg leave further to represent, that she declares, she is several months advanced in her pregnancy, for which reason she humbly desires, that her execution may be respited till she shall have brought forth.

Worcester
May 20, 1778

Bathsheba looked up to Maccarty. "I misjudged you, Reverend," she said. "Forgive me. Thank you." She called to Mrs Curtis for a quill and ink. With the Reverend as a witness, she carefully signed "Bathshua" under Ross's signature, then misspelled her married name. "It distresses me to write it," she explained as she inserted the missing "n."

"Why 'Bathshua'?" the Reverend asked.

"I prefer it. My family and my closest friend have always called me that, or 'Shua.' My husband insisted on 'Bathsheba.' He thought 'Bathshua' was trivial and sentimental, and 'Shua' even worse. But now he's dead." She pointed to Maccarty's note. "May I add to this?"

He nodded.

"*The above application is made at my most earnest request and wish.*" She signed again, this time correctly.

"Will the Councilors heed us, do you think?" Unlikely. After all, she was the daughter of a notorious enemy of the people. "The Councilors, Reverend, can you go over them with me?"

He had taken pains to make the necessary inquiries. "According to Council rules, the eldest member present at any given meeting acts as president," he explained. "Eldest in terms of service, that is. Lately the office has shifted back and forth between Judge Jeremiah Powell and Artemus Ward, with Ward serving only for short interim periods when Powell is away."

"Jeremiah Powell! That lifts my spirit." She explained how he had hired Nathan and then later, after Nathan's arrest, had arranged for his release from gaol. He probably would listen with an open mind.

"We can thank God for that." But, on the other hand, the Reverend continued, Artemus Ward was well known for his puritanical beliefs. There would be no leniency there. "And don't underestimate the power of John Avery. In him might lie a serious snag." Deputized by Sam Adams as Secretary of the Council, Avery had a long and strong connection with the rebel cause, beginning with his involvement with Adams' Loyal Nine, the core group of the Sons of Liberty. He was generally believed to have been an instigator of the Stamp Act Riots in August, '65: the hanging of Andrew Oliver in effigy, the trashing of the Oliver shop, and the gutting of Hutchinson's ancestral home on Garden Court Street. Later, behind the scenes, he led the mob that desecrated Andrew Oliver's funeral. "And right now," the Reverend added, "he chairs a committee that is drawing up a roster of Loyalists to be exiled forever from the State of Massachusetts Bay. Your father, I understand, will essentially head the list, preceded only by our former Loyalist magistrates, Governors Hutchinson and Bernard and Lieutenant Governor Thomas Oliver."

"No doubt. And there is more, Reverend, something not so generally known. Sarah Briggs Spooner, my husband's stepmother, who raised him, re-married after Joshua's father died. The groom was John Avery's father, a recent widower."

"Something of the kind has been whispered about." The Reverend paused to think. "John Avery, then, is Mr Spooner's stepbrother, from what you say." He shook his head. "Not good."

"No, but perhaps not as important as it seems." She was grasping at a straw. "Although Joshua and John were close in age, they weren't close otherwise. I can't recall my husband ever even mentioning John Avery. I knew of their relationship only because my father told me.

He didn't like it, to be linked in any way with such a blatant Patriot. But he was willing to discount it because, I guess, he knew that Joshua and Avery didn't get along."

Maccarty started to speak, got up, sat down again.

"Reverend, tell me what you're thinking. I have great need to know."

"I hesitate, I dislike being so discouraging, but you have asked, and so perhaps I should suggest that you not put too much stock in the prior lack of intimacy between those two men. Family bonds may well take ascendance now. Revenge can be a powerful force, and no matter how you look at it, you are a convicted murderer of John Avery's step brother. And Avery's influence will carry a lot of weight."

"Yes. I fear it's going to be like trying to stop the wind," she said. "Oh, Reverend, for God's sake, offer me a word of hope!"

"Pray God that Avery's judgment—or that of any Councilman— will not be clouded."

"Pray God."

Chapter 31

The Reverend went immediately to Boston to deliver the petitions. Radiating righteousness, Artemus Ward met him in the Council chamber, sternly accepted the documents, and dismissed him. In his younger days, when Ward was Shrewsbury's representative in the General Court, he had sided with James Otis and Sam Adams against the Brigadier, and later, when hostilities began, he was made Commander-in-Chief of Massachusetts' military forces, in charge at the Battle at Bunker's Hill. When the Continental Congress handed the command of the Continental Army to George Washington, Ward took on lesser military assignments until 1777, when ill health forced him to give up army life, and move into civil service for the rebel cause. To this new mission he brought strong convictions about right and wrong.

It was with some anxiety, therefore, that Maccarty waited day after day without word from the Council. Then, just when he'd decided he could wait no longer, a courier brought two officially stamped documents, with instructions that the Reverend deliver them to Sheriff William Greenleaf. One of these moved the date of the execution forward from June fourth until the second of July. The other was a *Writ de Ventre Inspiciendo*:

> *We, the Revolutionary Council of Massachusetts Bay, being desirous of knowing the truth of Bathsheba Spooner's Representation that she is quick with child, do command you William Greenleaf, to take with you two men midwives, and twelve discreet and lawful matrons of your County, to be first duly sworn, then to go to the said Bathsheba Spooner, and cause her diligently to be*

176

searched by the said matrons, in the presence of the said men midwives, by the Breasts and Belly, and certify the truth whether she be quick with child or not, and if she be quick with child, how long she has so been. Return their findings under your seal, and the seals of the said men midwives at or before the 25th day of June next, together with the names of the matrons by whom you shall cause the said search and inspection to be made; hereof fail not.

> *Witness the Major part of the Council of Massachusetts Bay in New England, at Boston, this twenty-eighth day of May A.D. 1778.*

> *By their Honors' Order,*
> *John Avery, D'y Sec'y*

The news about the *Writ* spread rapidly. Some people said that Mrs Spooner's claim of pregnancy was a hoax, the sort of thing one might expect of a loose woman; others maintained that it constituted proof that she'd had an adulterous affair with Ross, who was generally perceived as a victim of seduction. He had become the object of considerable sympathy, for everybody knew about his piety and recent baptism. Moreover, he was said to have received a glorious manifestation of the grace of God, a true redemption. Even his Ipswich sweetheart, heavy with a child he did not deny was his, journeyed all the way to Worcester to forgive him.

While the gossips speculated about the nature and extent of Mrs Spooner's sins, Sheriff Greenleaf set about his duty of choosing the twelve matrons to examine her. But he took his time. He had been convinced by Mrs Spooner, as well as Mrs Curtis and the Reverend Maccarty, that she told the truth, and he reasoned that the longer he put off the test the better, since her condition would only become more obvious with time. So it wasn't till the second week in June that he got the group together and took them to the gaol, along with two men midwives to serve as witnesses. He asked the women to wait with Mrs Curtis until he summoned them, one by one, starting with Sarah Jones, a good-wife of about Bathsheba's age.

"Bare your breasts," the matron ordered.

Bathsheba glanced at the men midwives, clearly as ill at ease as she was. Sheriff Greenleaf turned away, and stood staring through the bars of the cell door, clenching his hands behind his back. Now and then he cleared his throat.

The matron told Bathsheba to get on with it and pushed her roughly toward the window. With an unclean hand, the woman squeezed a breast, and, her face thrust close, she peered at the skin around the nipples. "Not the color I'd expect a breeding woman to have," she muttered. "Stand against the wall." She pulled up Bathsheba's skirt and probed her belly. "When and how did this thing you claim you're carrying get started?"

Bathsheba threw back her head, teeth clenched and defiant. This was even more degrading than she had expected. She would never have allowed it had she not been absolutely certain that the findings would give her child a chance to live.

The matron glanced at the men midwives, shook her head almost imperceptibly, and waited for the Sheriff to dismiss her. Another woman was admitted, and another, until they all had pushed and probed, some more gently than others.

Bathsheba buttoned her bodice, smoothed her skirt, and spoke softly to the sheriff. "May I sit down now, please?" Greenleaf offered her the stool, and held out his hand. She took it gratefully.

Hours later, the Reverend Maccarty came to tell her that the women had unanimously agreed that she was not quick with child. "Are you certain that you bear a foetus that is mature enough to be alive" he asked.

178

"Absolutely!" What right had he to doubt? "Those women *must* have felt it." She seized the bars at her cell window and yanked at them, seething with anger and frustration.

"In your case, the facts are less important than the prejudice against you," the Reverend said. "You are seen only as a woman totally depraved."

Bathsheba turned on him. "A lot of good your promises and prayers! Go on home to your chamber and beseech your God with some easier requests than those on my behalf."

Maccarty merely shook his head.

She blazed at him. "Go! Get out!"

Alone, Bathsheba gave way to anguish. She was helpless with rage, and not until many hours later was she calm enough to plan. Slowly a resolve emerged from the tangle in her mind: she simply would not accept defeat. Her thoughts kept coming back to Jeremiah Powell. He had headed the list of the thirteen Council members who had signed the order to delay the execution and he had seniority on the Council, often serving as its president. He might help, he had helped Nathan, he *would* help! His sense of justice would prompt him to intervene. If only she could talk with Nathan, ask him to lay her case before Judge Powell, but that was not possible. Since her conviction, she had been denied contact with everyone outside the gaol except her family and the Reverend. She certainly would not be allowed to see or write to a man known for his Loyalist leanings. She would have to act herself.

She therefore immediately started to compose a new petition to the Councilors, couched in terms of suitable humility—humility she did not feel.

May it please your honors: with unfeigned gratitude I acknowledge the favor you lately granted me, of a reprieve. I must beg, once more, humbly to lie at your feet, and to represent to you, that though the jury of matrons, that were appointed to examine my case, have not brought in my favor, yet that I am absolutely certain

179

of being in a pregnant state, and above four months advanced in it; and that the infant I bear was lawfully begotten. I am earnestly desirous of being spared, till I shall be delivered of it. I must humbly desire your honors, notwithstanding my great unworthiness, to take my deplorable case into your compassionate consideration. What I bear, and clearly perceive to be animated, is innocent of the faults of her who bears it, and has, I beg leave to say, a right to the existence which God hath begun to give it. Your honors' humane christian principles, I am very certain, must lead you to desire to preserve life, even in this its miniature state, rather than to destroy it. Suffer me, therefore, with all earnestness, to beseech your honors to grant me such a further length of time, at least, as that there may be the fairest and fullest opportunity to have the matter fully ascertained—and as in duty bound, shall, during my short continuance, pray.

Bathshua Spooner
Worcester Gaol
June 16th, 1778

Bathsheba gave the letter to Maccarty when he visited that evening. He read it carefully and nodded his approval. "I'll see that it gets sent by special messenger," he said.

The Councilors received Bathsheba's petition in time to consider it in conjunction with the matrons' unfavorable report, but they were not swayed. Her word weighed as nothing against the claims of the women. Even Judge Powell's urgent plea for reconsideration fell on deaf ears. The warrant for Mrs Spooner's execution would stand as formerly decreed, to go forward on the second of July, 1778.

While waiting for the Council to reply, Bathsheba thought carefully and clearly about what steps she would take should her petition be denied, and, in her fierce determination not to let the Council win, she came upon a way to achieve an ultimate victory. She therefore was prepared when the news arrived, and she forthwith demanded to see sister Mary's husband, Dr Green. He greeted her with an embrace, bringing love from Mary. He told her of their plan to inter her body on the Green estate when the ordeal was over. "No one but the family shall ever know the spot," he promised. "It's Mary's dearest wish that you shall rest in peace." Bathsheba knew that she could count on him.

"I asked you to come," she said, "because I have two requests, and I earnestly desire that you will grant them. I want to try once more, and I need your help."

"Yes?"

"You are a man of wealth and stature, held in great respect all over Worcester County. People listen when you speak. I think the men who witnessed my examinations are honest in their hearts, but they let public sentiment and the dishonest, spiteful matrons overwhelm them. Much as I hate the thought of strangers groping again at my person, I want the men-midwives to examine me themselves. Also Hannah Mower, a woman midwife Mrs Curtis recommends. I want you to do so also, to certify that the findings are correct. You must first persuade the Sheriff to allow it, and then have the courage to inform the Council of the results."

Stunned, John Green sat down on the cot beside her.

"I know that opinion is so much against me that, if you do what I request, your reputation will be threatened. I know that I am asking a great deal, but an innocent life depends on it."

The doctor faced her, admiration in his eyes. "Strength like steel," he said. "I cannot but be obliged to try to match it. Moreover, to say 'no' would be wrong, and Mary never would forgive me. I fear, though, that facts are not important here. The Council is weary of your case."

"You will find that I am carrying a living child. There will be no room for doubt. I agree that no matter what evidence is laid before them, those men will probably not change their minds. But I want to give them one more chance."

181

John nodded. "Yes. And your second request?"

"If, as both you and I expect, the Council still refuses to let me live until the child is born, I want you and colleagues of your choice, in the presence of the Sheriff and other witnesses, to cut my body open after I am hanged. Remove the child. Announce and document its sex and age. Then bury us together."

Let the message toll down through centuries.

Chapter 32

While Bathsheba was making her requests to Dr Green, the Reverend Maccarty was writing yet another letter to the Councilmen:

May it please the Honorable Board,

The news arrived last evening that Mrs Spooner's petition for a reprieve was not granted. People that are acquainted with her circumstances are accordingly affected with it. I am myself fully satisfied of her being in a pregnant state, & have been so for a considerable time. And it is with deep regret that I think of her being cut off, till she shall have bro't forth, which will eventually, though not intentionally, be destroying innocent life. An experienced midwife here visited her this week, & examined her, & found her quick with child—Wherefore, tho' I think justice ought to take place upon her as well as the rest, yet I might beg leave earnestly to desire that she might be respited at least for such time as that the matter may be fully cleared up—And I have no doubt it will be so satisfactorily to everyone.

I write this, may it please your honors, of my own accord, not at her desire, for I have not seen her since the news arrived.

I should be very sorry if your honors should consider me as over-assiduous in this matter—But principles of humanity, of Christianity, & a desire that righteousness

> *may go forth, have powerfully prompted me to make this
> application on her behalf.*
>
> *I beg leave with all dutiful respect to subscribe, your
> Honors' most dutiful & most humble servant,*
>
> *Thaddeus Maccarty*
> *Worcester*
> *June 26ᵗʰ, 1778*

Maccarty's letter arrived in Boston the same afternoon as Dr Green's unsolicited report, which stated that the undersigned—John Green, Josiah Wilder, Elijah Dix, and Hannah Mower, all experienced in midwifery—had re-examined Mrs Spooner, and had reason to believe that she was indeed quick with child. A third document, sent by two of the original, determined matrons, contradicted Dr Green's assessment. When they heard of his Committee, they had taken it upon themselves to seek permission to re-examine Mrs Spooner, and they wrote that their findings confirmed their conviction that she did not bear a living foetus.

Sheriff Greenleaf waited, postponing the erection of the gallows in the hope that only three would be required on the second of July. But no word came from Boston, no sign, and by Thursday morning he could no longer put things off. He ordered that four gibbets be erected on a scaffold on the outskirts of town in an open field large enough to hold the myriad spectators flooding into Worcester from all over Massachusetts.

Bathsheba lay on her cot, grey with pain; the slightest movement tortured her. *My last twilight*, she thought, as she watched the changing light slanting through the bars of her cell window. But the focus of her consciousness was not on the misery of her body or the awful certainties that lay ahead. Instead she was consumed by her loathing for the men in Boston who could not wait, who lusted for her execution with such obscene avidity that they would rather kill her child than countenance a delay.

Mrs Curtis came to tell her that the Reverend Maccarty was outside. "He'd like to see you, ma'am. He says he won't intrude for long, unless, of course, you'd like for him to stay."

Bathsheba made an effort to sit up. "The fault lies with the matrons who last examined me," she told him when he asked concerning her infirmity. "They did what they should not have done. And now, because of their false witness, a child will die before its earthly life outside my womb begins." She paused to recover from her exertion while he prayed silently. Then, "My physical condition is degrading. It will be all that I can do to stand tomorrow, much less walk the short distance to the Meeting House to hear your execution sermon. I know I must forego it." Her face turned ashen as a cramp knifed through her. When it passed, she tried to smile. "I was looking forward to the inspiration of your words and the comfort they would bring," she said.

Maccarty took a little notebook from his pocket, tore out several pages, and placed them within her reach on the floor beside the cot. "These are the notes for the part of my sermon that I intended to direct to you alone," he said. He took her hand and held it for a moment. "God be with you. Try to get some sleep."

She attempted to get up to see him out. It's the least that I can do, she thought; he has done so much for me.

He indicated with a gesture that she should not try, and he eased her back onto the cot. He turned her pillow to a fresh, cool surface, smoothed it, and lowered her head. "Good night," he said. "God rest you well."

Before he left the gaol, he spoke to Mrs Curtis, asking her to take a candle to Mrs Spooner's cell. "She should not be left in darkness," he advised. "And please prepare for her an herbal potion laced heavily with opium."

Bathsheba lay still. Mosquitoes, attracted by the candlelight, droned through the window. The shrill vibrations of cicadas in the fields mingled with the voices of the people lingering outside the tavern by the gaol yard. She could make out scraps of talk: four felons to be hanged, and one a woman. Yes, a woman and an unborn child. She reached for the pages from Maccarty's notebook, and as she strained to read his tiny script by the flickering light, she could almost hear his voice urging her to call on God, even at the final hour. "We know that if we confess our sins, the blood of Jesus can cleanse us from unrighteousness. We know the story of the penitent thief upon the cross. I pray that, before you are required to step up to the gallows, you too can see your way to bow down before the Lord with true repentance. But perhaps you have already made your peace with Him. Can it be that it is thus with you, poor dying woman?"

Yes, almost. Over the past few days, her solitary musings had come together with the Reverend's counseling to create a guiding spiritual presence. Now she was no longer certain that Joshua had had no right to live, she was no longer filled with bitterness. Perhaps he couldn't help himself, just as she could not. As a kind of prayer, her first since childhood, she murmured her regrets for her traffic with the Devil. "May God have mercy and save the child I am carrying."

She sipped the toddy Mrs Curtis brought, then closed her eyes.

At noon the following day, the largest congregation the Reverend Maccarty had ever served crowded into Old South Meeting House. A storm was brewing, greying the white-washed interior and accenting the hush that greeted Buchanan, Brooks, and Ross as their guards escorted them to a front pew. Then a wave of whispers: where was Mrs Spooner? What kind of ruse was she up to now? Maybe she'd been let off at the last minute.

"Mrs Spooner is too ill to join us," the Reverend announced before opening the service with a psalm. Ignoring the cries of children, bedeviled by humidity and heat and frightened by the somber atmosphere, he called for everyone to join in the general confession.

He delivered his sermon quietly. "Because the murderers have sinned, their temporal lives must be destroyed. Blood for blood." He gave examples from the Bible, proving by the word of God that the criminals must give their lives to atone for their taking of another's. Toward the end, he spoke directly to the convicted men, expanding on the justice of their sentence, but assuring them that, as black a crime as murder is, they would be redeemed through Christ's Atonement if they were as truly penitent as they seemed. He finished with a parable. "We read in the Bible of the servant who came in at the eleventh hour, and yet received the same wages as those who bore the heat and burden of the day."

After the service, the Reverend went immediately to the gaol, followed by his brethren who had come from towns throughout the state. He paused before he entered and, turning to them, requested that they wait outside.

He found Bathsheba sitting by her window, pale and calm, dressed in a lustrous grey silk gown provided by her mother. "Mrs Curtis has been kind," she said. "She let me sleep until the opium wore off, then gave me a morning potion to further dull the pain and soften my awareness. She helped me dress."

For a final time, the Reverend asked again if she was willing to be baptized.

"I am," she answered. "At last I have a great, sincere desire for that."

His smile and expression of relief made clear how important her decision was to him. He murmured a prayer of thanks, and, without asking her to rise, performed the simple ceremony, with Mrs Curtis and the Sheriff bearing witness,

"I pray God this means my unborn child is baptized too," she said. "And will be with me in heaven."

Sheriff Greenleaf gently lowered the noose over her head, and the Reverend drew her long black hair out of the loop, letting it fall freely on her shoulders. She touched the rope. "I esteem this as much as though it were a necklace of gold or diamonds," she said. The end of torment; she was glad.

"Mrs Spooner can't walk through this heat," Maccarty informed the sheriff. "I beg you give me leave to take her in my chaise."

Greenleaf nodded his assent.

Church bells knelled as the procession crawled through the sultry meadow under the guard of a hundred men. Buchanan, Brooks, and Ross walked behind four horse-drawn pine coffins. The crowd pressed close. Horses pawed and whinnied. Thunder sounded in the distance.

Seated beside the Reverend, Bathsheba struggled with her pain, thrust deeper by each rut that rocked the chaise. She managed nods to acquaintances scattered throughout a sea of strangers, Hardwick folks whom she'd known long ago, come to see her be cut off. She was sorry now that she had begged her family to stay away. "Mama," she had said, "I cannot bear to have you watch this indecent act, in which I am the featured player." But now that it was happening, she felt terribly alone.

Then, through the lowering darkness of the threatening storm, she made out Uncle John, standing on a nearby hillock. Nathan was there beside him, and he raised his hand in a gesture that seemed more like a greeting than farewell, telling her his spirit was with her. Uncle John bent forward and reached out as if longing to embrace her. She yearned for them and waved and they waved back. Her pain gave way a little, and a transcending calm came over her.

The soldiers were already on the stage, listening to the Sheriff read their warrant. Ross prayed out loud, and the others spoke in murmurs muffled by the rumbling clouds. Forks of lightning streaked from heaven to horizon, followed by mighty thunder.

The Reverend Maccarty helped Bathsheba from the chaise. When she stood up, she felt a thick, sticky trail of blood ooze down her thighs, and fear possessed her that her dress was stained. The Reverend took her arm, then stood by, steadying the ladder as she started up the thirteen steps on hands and knees. Once on the stage, she found the strength to stand and take her place beside the soldiers.

She whispered she was ready. "I doubt not that it will be well with me," she told the Sheriff. "And with the infant I am carrying."

With eyes that betrayed his anguish, he fastened all four nooses to the gallows, and from his pocket took a large, black handkerchief to signal it was time.

Panic. What think? What do? She searched the crowd for Nathan, as far as she could see, and spotted him leading Uncle John, weeping, from the spectacle. The Reverend, too, had turned away, refusing to bear witness. The Sheriff hooded her as a cascade of thunder burst again, and, with a reverberating crack, the world split open.

Like a black velvet curtain at play's end, Bathsheba's consciousness shut down.

The truth spread rapidly, silencing the drenched, dispersing crowd: Dr Green and two colleagues had opened Mrs Spooner and taken from her a foetus, lifeless but still warm, of approximately five months' growth.

When news of this reached Boston, leaders of the State of Massachusetts Bay tore out a page from the Revolutionary Council's Record Book and closed it.

Epilogue

An account of what happened to the other real-life characters in the book after the executions

In October, 1778, the long-standing controversy between Jonathan Danforth (Nathan) and Hardwick officials over his status as a Tory was resolved by action of the Massachusetts House of Representatives. It decreed that Danforth must never again bring suit against Hardwick's Select Men or Committee, as he did in 1776 after getting out of jail; they, in turn, were ordered to leave him alone and return the property they had confiscated. A year after Danforth's first wife, Susanna, died in November, 1779, he married Bathsheba's cousin, Anna Ruggles, and about this time he moved his family to Barre, a town adjacent to Hardwick. After the war, Danforth returned with his family to Hardwick and subsequently served as a Select Man, Assessor, and Tax Collector. But he never forgot his conflicts with those in power during the Revolution. We find in Lucius Paige's *History of Hardwick* the following story: "In 1831, when he [Danforth] was eighty-eight years old, Colonel Stephen Rice, a member of the Revolutionary Committee of Correspondence, died, at the age of ninety-five. Soon afterwards, Mr Goldsbury [Danforth's pastor] called on Mr Danforth, who recounted some of his early trials and sufferings. Among other grievances, he said the Committee of Correspondence prohibited him from leaving his own farm, except to go to meeting on Sundays, and to attend funerals. 'One day,' he said, 'a member of the Committee informed me there was to be a funeral, and inquired whether I wished to be present; I told him I always liked to go to funerals, and I hoped I might live to attend the funerals of the whole Committee; and I have done it; I have seen every divil of them under ground; Rice was the last of them." Danforth himself died in September, 1833, aged ninety, his wife Anna having preceded him by eleven years. Together they had seven children.

Brigadier General Timothy Ruggles and other prominent Loyalists continued throughout the war to make unsuccessful efforts to get permission from British Headquarters to raise Loyalist American troops. Some historians have attributed the failure of these attempts to jealousies among the higher officers. For example, it has been suggested that General Clinton refused even to discuss the matter with Ruggles because he had discovered that the Brigadier was writing to influential men in London sharply criticizing the British high command in America. Whatever the reason, the two men were openly at loggerheads, and one can imagine that Clinton did everything he could to thwart the Brigadier's ambitions.

On October 16, 1778, the Brigadier's name appeared, along with Governors Bernard and Hutchinson and Lieutenant Governor Andrew Oliver, at the top of the list of men exiled for good from Massachusetts. Six months later his estate was formally confiscated, although his son Timothy managed to get permission to occupy the house rent-free. By September, 1779, most of Ruggles' large and scattered properties had been sold at auction.

The Brigadier was living in Newton Creek, Long Island, when Cornwallis surrendered at Yorktown in October, 1781. From his signature on a dated legal document, we know that he was still in New York on November 8, 1782. But sometime between then and July of the next year (probably in April, when thousands of Loyalist refugees were evacuated from New York), he went to Nova Scotia with his sons John and Richard. In accordance with his request to the Crown, he was granted ten thousand acres of land east of Granville, stretching across the hilly peninsula to the Bay of Fundy. Eventually he received partial compensation for his Hardwick losses (only about a quarter of the £19,501 he applied for), and about £150 annual pension for his service as a Mandamus Councilor under General Gage. With these assets he set about creating a new showplace, which he called *Roseway*. He situated his house overlooking the Annapolis Valley, facing south on the slopes of a hill which soon became known as Ruggles Mountain (now Phinney Mountain). Perhaps with sentimental longing for his homeland, he imported Quincy granite for the foundation. For his orchard he had every stone and root removed to a depth of about three feet over an area of close to an acre, on which he planted fruit trees and seedlings sent from Hardwick by his son Timothy. He terraced a gulch on his property, locally referred to as "the vault," which faced south and was therefore ideally situated to catch the heat. There he planted a variety of exotic fruit and nut trees, normally thought to be suited only to a southern climate. To his neighbors' astonishment, these plantings flourished.

It was in the vault, while he was showing visitors around, that he accidentally slipped and suffered a severe rupture of an old hernia. He died a few days later, on August 4, 1795, in his eighty-fifth year, and was buried in the yard of Pine Grove Church in Central Wilmot, Nova Scotia. Much later, a monument to his memory was erected in the Middleton cemetery by Eliza Bayard West, a great-granddaughter from Minnesota.

The Brigadier left his properties in Nova Scotia to his sons. Holdings in Vermont, granted by the King and never confiscated, were divided among Bathsheba's children and her sisters, Mary, Martha, and Elizabeth.

Bathsheba's mother, Bathsheba Bourne Newcomb Ruggles (Sheba), remained in Hardwick with her son Timothy until her death in 1787, aged eighty-three. She is buried in the old cemetery in Hardwick, across from the Common, near the Town Hall, her grave marked with a simple marble tablet of a relatively recent date.

John Ruggles (Uncle John), cited in Paige's *History of Hardwick* as being "very eccentric, perhaps partially insane, but harmless," moved from New Braintree to Rochester, Massachusetts, where his father, the Reverend Timothy Ruggles, had been pastor from 1710 till 1768. John died unmarried in 1815, aged eighty-four.

Timothy Ruggles Jr remained in Hardwick until after his mother's death, residing on the homestead which, though confiscated in 1779, was afterwards released to him by the Commonwealth. In 1789 he sold the farm and moved to Granville, Nova Scotia with his wife Sarah and several of his younger children. There he became a prominent citizen, and died in 1832 at the age of nearly 93; Sarah lived on until 1842, and died aged 92.

John and Richard Ruggles were both on the list of Tories banished from Massachusetts in October, 1778. John, and probably Richard also, served the British cause on both Staten Island and Long Island, as well as in Rhode Island, where John joined a Loyalist corps led by Edward Winslow Jr of Plymouth. The outfit successfully harassed the rebels up and down the New England coast for months. After the war, both John and Richard joined their father in Nova Scotia, where each received 800 acres from the Crown. Richard died about 1834, aged 90; John lived till "an old age."

Martha Ruggles Tufts, who lived in Brookfield on the south side of Post Road, not far from the Spooners, died there in 1813, aged 76. Her gravestone is near Joshua's in the Tufts family plot.

Mary Ruggles Green lived with her husband Dr John Green on their 180-acre Worcester homestead until she died in June, 1814, aged 73. Many of their descendants became prominent in New England and New York politics. The Green estate remained in the Green family for five generations until it was purchased by the city of Worcester in 1905 at the cost of $54,900, towards which the Green heirs contributed $50,000. For years the Green Hill Park Mansion served not only as a place for social events, but also as a museum containing curios from all over the world, including stuffed examples of every species of New England bird. As an economic measure, Worcester's Park and Recreation Commission tore down the mansion in the middle of the twentieth century. Green Hill Park itself still remains

(2003). Portraits of both John and Mary Green hang in the Hardwick Historical Museum.

Although Elizabeth Ruggles Chandler left Massachusetts for England with her husband Gardner before her sister was executed, they both returned when the war was over. Along with her sisters and Bathsheba's children, she inherited property in Bennington, Vermont from her father. Her husband purchased Dummer Farm in Brattleboro, Vermont, and they lived there with their three children, Sarah, Elizabeth Augusta, and Charles, from 1789 until 1795.

Bathsheba's children, Elizabeth and her siblings Josh and Baby Bath, were made wards of Joshua's nephew, John Jones Spooner, who abandoned his responsibilities as guardian and left Massachusetts in 1784. By that time, Elizabeth was almost of age, and on December 18, 1789, she married William Heath, Jr, son of Major General William Heath, who had served with distinction under General Washington. A letter, written in February, 1792, from General Heath to Joseph Dorr, Judge of the Probate Court in Worcester, supports his son's application to be made administrator of the Spooner estate, and laments its deplorable condition, with "debts to a considerable amount, on interest which is daily increasing, while several years' rents on the real estate remain uncollected." Elizabeth died in 1820, aged 53.

According to the same letter from General William Heath (Elizabeth Spooner's father-in-law) to Judge Joseph Dorr, Joshua Spooner Jr went to sea in 1790 when he was twenty years old. He died in London in 1801.

Bathsheba Spooner (Baby Bath) was only fourteen in 1789 when her guardian, John Jones Spooner, left Massachusetts. At that time she chose to become the ward of her mother's cousin, Nathaniel Ruggles of Roxbury. On October 18, 1798 she married Peter Trott, a Boston watchmaker, with whom she had two daughters. After his death in 1805, she married Dr Sewell Heyward in 1807. In her latter years her mind became increasingly troubled, and in 1856 she was put in the custody of Mathias Crocker. She died in Cambridge on June 1, 1858, aged 83.

In 1782, all three Spooner children received one half of the rents from the Oliver estate in Middleborough, which had been confiscated in 1775. This transfer came about through a petition to the General Court by their guardian, John Jones Spooner. Half of the Oliver estate had been mortgaged to Joshua for his loan of a thousand pounds to Judge Peter Oliver's three sons back in 1765.

Although Ephriam Cooley's Tavern figures in this book as early as 1766, it actually was not built until 1777. Cooley remained in Brookfield until his death in January, 1825, aged 83.

The Reverend Thaddeus Maccarty continued as minister of Old South Meeting House until his death on July 20, 1784, aged 63. All told, he spent 37 years as a beloved pastor there.

In 1779 Levi Lincoln was designated to prosecute the claims of the new government against Loyalists whose estates had been confiscated under the Absentee Act. In 1797 he became a member of the Massachusetts senate. Afterwards he was elected to the seventh Congress of the United States, but he was no sooner sworn in than newly elected President Thomas Jefferson appointed him Attorney General of the United States, an office that he held for four years. He then served as the Lieutenant Governor of Massachusetts. In 1811, he was offered but declined an appointment as an Associate Justice of the Supreme Court of the United States. The founder of a family whose name is still well known in Worcester, he died there on April 14, 1820, aged 71.

Robert Treat Paine remained the Attorney General of Massachusetts until 1790, when he became a judge on the Supreme Judicial Court of Massachusetts, a post he held until 1804. A statue of him, bearing an inscription noting that he was a signer of the Declaration of Independence, stands across from City Hall in Taunton,

Massachusetts, where he lived from 1761 until 1780. He died in Boston on May 11, 1814, aged 83, and is buried there in the historic Granary Burial Ground.

William Cushing, who presided at Bathsheba's trial, held the office of Chief Justice of the Superior Court of Judicature in Massachusetts until 1789, when he was promoted to the Supreme Court of the United States. In 1787 he also chaired the Massachusetts Convention called to act on the adoption of the Federal Constitution. While John Jay, the first Chief Justice of the nation's Supreme Court, was in Europe negotiating the treaty with Great Britain (1794), Cushing took his place *pro tem*. On Jay's resignation, Cushing was nominated and unanimously confirmed as the new Chief Justice, but his health was failing and he declined the honor. He continued as Associate Justice until his death in 1810.

Jedediah Foster, the only judge at the trial known to Bathsheba (according to the novel), was on the Committee to draft the Massachusetts Constitution with John Adams, but he died in October, 1779, before the work was done. The Reverend Nathan Fiske, who preached Joshua Spooner's funeral sermon, also gave the eulogy for Judge Foster, portraying him as a saintly man.

Except for records concerning the Spooner case, nothing was found concerning Sarah Stratten, Jesse Parker, Alexander Cummings, Dr Jonathan King, Ephriam Cooley, Reuben Olds, Mary Walker, Prudence, Captain Weldon, and Obediah Rice.

Selected Sources

American Antiquarian Society, Worcester, Massachusetts

Judge Jedediah Foster's notes on the trial

Various articles in the "Massachusetts Spy," (Spring, 1778), a phrase from one of which is used as the sub-title of this book

Sermons relative to the case delivered by the Reverend Parkman, the Reverend Maccarty, and the Reverend Fiske (*Sermon on the Tragical Death of Mr. Spooner*, delivered on March 3, 1778)

Parkman's diary (Parkman Family Papers 1707-1879, #1932)

"The Dying Declaration of James Buchanan, Ezra Ross, and William Brooks"

Levi Lincoln's notes, presumably used to present his case to the jury

Archives of the Commonwealth of Massachusetts, Columbia Point, Boston

All the documents relative to the Spooner Case to and from the Revolutionary Council, some of which are quoted in the book *verbatim*

Records of the Revolutionary Council, in the Revolutionary Council Papers, Vol. 168

John Spooner Sr's will

Massachusetts Historical Society, Boston

Robert Treat Paine's notes on the trial

Sibley's Harvard Graduates

The Boston Athenaeum

Peleg Chandler, "The Trial of Mrs. Spooner and Others," in *American Criminal Trials*, Vol. 2, Charles C. Little and James Brown, Boston, 1844, pp 3-58 and 375-383

The Hardwick Historical Museum

Lucius R. Paige, *History of Hardwick, Massachusetts, with a Genealogical Register*, Houghton, Mifflin & Co., New York, The Riverside Press, Cambridge, 1883

Various artifacts owned by Brigadier General Timothy Ruggles

Probate Court, Plymouth Massachusetts

Documents relating to the various Oliver estates

Printed in the United States
18102LVS00001B/106

9 781410 734006